Bound By Honor

By W. J. Lundy

© 2016 W. J. Lundy

Whiskey Tango Foxtrot
Bound By Honor

© 2016 W. J. Lundy

Cover Design by Andre Vasquez Junior

Editing: Terri King, Brittany King

Prologue

The hunt led him away from civilization, deep into the snow-covered valley. Stopping smoothly, he knelt down to check his back trail. His eyes drifted, tracking the moon through the thin veil of clouds. It would be dawn soon, and he was far from home. There were too many of them and he did not know what he would do if he found them. He searched the thick foliage and tall trees, zig zagging the terrain while looking for any sign of a trail.

His chest ached and his body was cold. With no time to grab a jacket, he'd been forced to move unprepared in pursuit of the camp's attackers. He stepped ahead and saw a human track; this one fresh, a heel print in the moist clay of the forest floor. Just ahead, a crumbling of rotted stump where a big boot kicked it then ground it down while the wearer stopped to look around. The young soldier studied the terrain. He knelt down and allowed his eyes to search, starting far out, then slowly sweeping to objects within his reach.

Grabbing a gloveful of the crumbling tree stump, he squeezed it, allowing the damp pieces to fall between his fingers. He reached out and cut a triangle into a nearby tree to mark his path. The ground flowed up and away from him, the trail following the natural contours in the ground. Most game trails moved that way. Wild animals traveled along paths of least resistance, and after generations of migration, they broke the earth, shaping the routes that he now followed. Recreational hikers probably once used this same path, compacting the clay and smoothing the surface. He suspected the raiders would follow the same route.

He rose back to his feet and felt the stiff muscles of his broad shoulders. He shrugged, flexing his back, and moved on. Dressed in tanned hides, he had left his worn and faded military clothing in a box months ago. His shirt was thick and well sewn; his canvas pants, soaked in wax and animal fat to make them waterproof. Having abandoned most of the things of his past, all that remained were his weapons. He carried an M9 pistol in a belt and an M4 he had recovered from a dead man.

Why did they come here? What reason would the raiders have to attack the camp? The people of Camp Cloud always kept to themselves. Nearly a year had passed since the Primal Holocaust; the beasts had moved to the background of their concerns. Hunger drove the Primals and their behavior was predictable—the living were what really scared the survivors; those that wanted what everyone else had. Dan Cloud, who led the group, managed to keep peace with other bands of survivors, trading when they could, but mostly just staying out of the way and hidden in their own remote mountain valley.

Shane stopped near a downed oak and leaned back, letting his weight rest on his heels. He looked again at the tough terrain. "I should stop now and dig in," he whispered. "Wait for help to catch up." They would for sure send a rescue party. He shook his head in frustration. What if they were all dead? What if there was no one coming?

"Impossible, they couldn't take them all; his people would come for them. They always come." Shane knelt again and let his finger touch the edges of a deep hoof print, squeezing bits of the damp soil in his hand. His stomach growled as he recognized the print. A big buck; it would make a fine meal for his fire. He looked up at the sky and saw the rising sun; he had been on the trail too long. He was burning out and losing his edge. He would give it another hour, and then secure shelter.

Crushed and bent vegetation off the trail reflected the light and caught his eye. Searching the battered weeds, he spotted a strange batch of tracks cutting the raiders' trail. He knew what they were, and it worried him more than his exhaustion. It was unusual to see Primals this far up the mountain, away from the easy traveling outside the valley. The infected monsters stayed away from the highlands unless they were hunting prey. Something either pushed them, or drew them there; most likely the gunfire from the attack.

Looking at the tracks, he could see there

were at least five of them, and one was a big son of a bitch by the way the worn boot tread pushed deep into the soil with every step. Shane stayed near the ground, listening for any sign they were close. He held his breath, exhaled slowly, and then took it in again, trying to taste the musty air. He did not move, becoming perfectly still. Hiding from the Primals was the same as stalking a deer—to stay hidden, you stayed motionless. Breathing lightly, Shane sat and patiently waited for a sign.

He looked up at the sky and back at the tracks; the rules were changing with the indication of Primals. He should move to high ground and seek shelter, find a place to hide until he was rested and more alert. He knew it was not good field craft to get arrogant on the trail, and wait until the last minute before finding safety.

Studying the Primal tracks, he could not tell how old they were; unlike the hoof prints, they could be fresh, a day old, or even older. In addition, the tracks went west, away from him. He swept his hand across the ground searching for more signs, but there was no indication they were doing anything more than passing across the range.

He scanned ahead and grimaced, testing even his own patience now. He would go just a bit farther, and if he found no sign of the raiders, he would stop and dig in. He would sleep and wait for the men from the camp to join him. He'd marked his path well and knew they would find him.

The game trail wound around and dipped into a ravine. At the bottom, he lost the raider tracks. Shane stepped back, eased into the thick underbrush, and then walked a half circle, looking for signs in the denser foliage— something that would indicate where the men jumped the trail. He found a broken branch, and a place where the grass bent in a different direction from that surrounding it. Shane froze, hearing the snort of a deer, and then a cry, followed by the sounds of bare fists pounding flesh. He edged away. The soldier knew he was in trouble.

Crouching low, he stalked back deeper into cover, trying to find a secure position to hide. Ahead, he spotted the flurry of activity at the same time he heard the low scream of an Alpha Primal. The Alphas were a special breed of infected that led the packs. More dominant, they somehow retained a human survival instinct and an ability to organize and direct what would — at first glance — appear to be a chaotic mob.

He watched as more of the screaming things joined the Alpha. Somehow, they had managed to corner the buck. The Alpha was already on it, attacking and lunging with fists, as others leapt at the deer, trying to drag it off its feet. Shane sympathized with the majestic animal, using its antlers to ward off more attackers as they joined in against it. He wanted to help, but this was not his fight. The deer was unable to flee, but refused to go down, even with the Alpha and several more holding it and swarming against it.

The soldier gripped the rifle tight, wanting to use it to put the animal out of its misery, but knowing that he could not. He lowered his head and backed away. He heard a loud exhale and a branch break behind him. The blood drained from Shane's cheeks. His muscles tensed, knowing he was in for a fight. He had pressed his luck too far. More leaves crunched to his rear, and he heard the sounds of feet rapidly beating the trail. Shane spun just as the first of the Primals leapt at him.

The young soldier rolled to his left, raising the rifle and getting off a single shot that knocked the first of his attackers away. His brain ran a sub-conscious count as they passed through his vison. *Five, one already down.* He raised the rifle to his shoulder as more closed the distance. He pulled the trigger, nothing; the carbine was jammed and he knew he would not get another shot off. He reached out and grabbed the barrel then swung with a two-handed grip, connecting with the next Primal and watching its jaw explode as it kissed the rifle stock. *Two down.* Shane tumbled forward and found his feet already scrambling ahead.

He was running for the ridge now, desperate to reach high ground. Swinging the rifle as he ran directly up the trail, leading the way with its stock, he connected straight on with the faces of his attackers. *Three — no, four down.* The deer behind him winced and whined, finally falling to the ground in a crash that sent the Primals into a frenzy.

Shane swung the rifle again, catching another. Although that hardly knocked it off course, the creature's neck snapped as its head wrenched to the side. He lost his footing and flew off the trail into a heavy thicket, a Primal tackling him from the side as they tumbled. *Where did that one come from?* He twisted as he rolled, entangled with the writhing Primal. Thorns snagged at his clothing and tore away at his skin. His head collided with the ground, causing a bright flash as his vision dimmed. Shane lost his grip on the rifle and fought to free his fighting knife from the scabbard. His own hands feeling clumsy, the muscle memory took over as his brain powered down.

Their roll stopped with him on the bottom, the short-barreled M4 hopelessly out of reach. The crazy mashed its open jaw into his left shoulder, biting deep. Shane screamed in pain as he drew back the knife. He smashed the blade down hard and drew back. Swinging again, he arced his arm and swung down with his right hand, delivering deep blows to the creature's back; shoving the metal into the Primal's lungs, twisting the hilt and searching for its heart. The Primal convulsed and shuddered a long, gurgling breath into the soldier's shoulder.

The dying the beast's weight settled heavy, pressing Shane to the forest floor. Pinned to the ground with only his right arm free, he let his head drop back. He heard the creatures down the ridge ripping the deer apart. He could feel his warm blood trickling down his neck and seeping toward the small of his back. As his vision faded and closed in, the dense trees above swam and rotated, he waited for more of them to mass on him. They would come, and he would not be able to fight them. He blinked his eyes, looking into the fading light.

He could not move his head; it was pinned to the side with his cheek pressed against the cold earth. Shane could smell the creature; the copper tang of the blood combined with the stench of the Primal filth caused his stomach to roil. He clenched his jaw, trying to hold back the retching. Fighting to calm his thoughts and to remain silent, he wondered why they had not attacked him yet. *Maybe I'm already dead. Maybe Ella is already dead; maybe they all are. Why did I come here? Why did I think following the raiders would make a difference?* He fought the temptation to quit as his body settled into the cold ground.

He tried to focus his ears only to hear the low groans and feasting sounds as the creatures consumed the buck. His stomach twisted. Dizzy and losing blood, he fought off the growing bile as his vision continued to blur. His shoulder ached with sharp pain. His head burned at the base of his skull where he hit his head in the fall. He struggled to breathe, the weight of the creature pressing on him. His vision tightened and closed up, his peripheral sight gone. Using the last of his strength, he attempted to roll the Primal off him, failing to budge it.

Shane took low breaths and fought to keep his eyes open. Listening to the Primals below, he was ready to face death; there was nothing left to do, his mind and body numb. Not wanting to be conscious when they attacked, he hoped he bled out before they came for him. He was tired. His thoughts clouded and ran together; he felt the cold ground below him. *It's okay, I'll just rest for a bit.* He released a long sigh and let his eyes close.

Chapter 1

**2 years after the fall.
The Outpost, Free Virginia Territories.**

The door slammed shut, blocking the cold wind from entering the room. Snow swirled around the big man and gathered at his feet. Wind whistled as it entered cracks in the ancient building. The large, broad-shouldered man stomped his feet, knocking snow from his worn leather boots. He turned and stripped a heavy fur coat from his shoulders before hanging it on a hook behind him. A slung MP5 sat tucked against his body in a handmade, deer hide holster. The air in the small room was dry and stank of filthy bodies and wood smoke.

A hunter sat alone in a dark corner, draining the last of his whiskey from a yellow-stained mason jar. He watched the large man move to the plank wood counter that ran along the back of the room. The other hunters in the room barely lifted their heads to acknowledge the entrance of the big man. He recognized him. He knew who the big man was; a good friend once, but one he'd neglected in recent times. Brad tried to think of how long it had been. It was the dead of winter now, and he was certain it had been summer when he'd last visited Camp Cloud down the valley near the mountain lake.

Brad preferred the outpost to Camp Cloud. This place was remote, high in the wilderness. He liked the seclusion of it, surrounded by tall pines and pressed into rough terrain. He kept telling himself this place was only a temporary stop on his way home. He looked down to the floor beside him and his already packed belongings then back up, watching the big man move across the room toward the bar. He wondered why the man was at the outpost; people from the Camp rarely traveled here.

Only a few others stayed in this secluded spot, the most distant position on Dan Cloud's property. The ones that lived here were hard types, those that had lost too much and did not like the constant reminders of the families they tried to forget. The men here gathered lumber and hunted for meat and furs. Some of them, however, just wasted away, hoping that one day, things would go back to the way there were before. The days before the fall. Days before the Primal virus took hold and destroyed civilization.

There were only two things on the menu in the old trappers' cabin-turned-tavern: salted venison and whiskey. The big man pressed against the counter and chose a jar of the latter. Then, he leaned back and searched the shadows. Tired, weary men occupied several of the tables; men looking for a spot to escape the brutal cold.

The big man's eyes scanned the darkness before settling on Brad. He smirked and turned back to order a second jar before approaching the table. He wended his way through the space and into the corner. He kicked a chair away from the table with a boot and sat down, placing the jars in front of him then sliding one across the table.

"You look like shit," the big man said.

Brad smiled, reaching across the table and taking the offered mason jar of homemade whiskey from his old friend. "I've been better," he answered. "What brings an unemployed SEAL all the way out here to Bachelor Town?"

Brooks shook his head. "Here on business." The man paused, seeing a stuffed rucksack with a rifle strapped to the top near Brad's feet. Brooks dipped his chin in the direction of the pack and said, "You going somewhere?"

Brad shrugged and sipped his whiskey. He had been planning for some time to make his way back home to Michigan. For the last week, he had spent the morning packing his gear, but only making it as far as the tavern. After a few drinks, he would change his mind and end up spending the rest of the day hunting or cutting wood. "Maybe," he said.

"You oughta move back to the main camp. No reason for you to live out here like this."

"This place suits me fine—just fine. I can hunt and fish. And hell, the booze isn't bad,"

Brad said taking a long pull from the jar. He finished it in a single swallow then raised his hand to the barkeep for another round.

Brooks laughed and shook his head. "You know you still have a chance with that girl, if that's what this is all about."

Brad's eyes grew big. "Who? Chelsea?"

"Yeah — what other girl could there be?"

Brad ignored the comment, flipping the empty jar upside down and pushing it away from him. He could feel the sweat on his back, the heat from the whiskey warming him even though it was the middle of February and the room was barely fifty degrees with a fire blazing in the wood stove. The bartender replaced the jar with a new one. Brad took it and sipped this time before placing it back on the table. "So how is she? Still with Shane, I imagine."

Brooks laughed again, his tone noticeably irritating Brad. The big man drank from his own jar and looked Brad in the eye. "She was never with Shane. Shane is like a brother to her; like a brother to all of us. Is that why you came out here? After all the shit we've been through, is that what you're hiding from?"

Brad looked away. "I assume you made the trip out here for something more than to pester me about my living conditions."

The big man nodded and stroked his long beard. "Sean sent me. We have Rangers in camp; they're putting a patrol together and need our help."

"Rangers? Texas or Army?" Brad asked.

"Texas."

Brad grunted and took another pull from the jar. After the fall of the government during the *Battle of the Meat Grinder* at Washington D.C. and later following the death of the president, the nation broke up into small, defensible regions. Most of what was once considered the traditional state leadership went north, taking surviving remnants of the National Guard with them. These small groups helped to reinforce Ohio, Indiana, northern Wisconsin, and Michigan, with parts of western Pennsylvania, forming a geographic safe haven. This new Mid-West Alliance used the Great Lakes and the Ohio River as natural barriers, and eventually were able to purge great regions of the infected Primals.

As the world degraded, the southwest retracted, forming a new border region encompassing Texas, Oklahoma, Mexico, and Arizona. Already home to a great deal of the nation's military might, they used the armed forces and remaining fuel reserves to their advantage. Many generals and base commanders around the United States closed their own facilities and eventually joined the United States of Texas. This southwestern province was now home to most of the nation's previous populations, and were in control of the only viable Primal vaccine.

The wild card was with the remnants of the Department of Homeland Security. High-level heads of state, government employees, and parts of the military broke off and went to bunkers in the Rocky Mountains. Calling themselves the Coordinated National Response Team, the C.N.R.T. considered themselves the new central government. They posted up in the center of the Greater Colorado Nations and attempted to keep control over smaller regions by force with the might of the US Military. Slowly, the C.N.R.T. began making rash decisions to cut off support to remote settlements within the former United States.

These unpopular decisions created mutinies with military units still loyal to the people, causing many of them to defect to Texas. The C.N.R.T. went dark just after the discovery of a vaccine for the Primal virus. All communications with their bunkers ended, and nobody had heard from them in some time. With the fall of the C.N.R.T., Colorado and most of the military elements still under their control scattered with survivors and joined the two remaining regions.

With the country and most of the world in shambles, the United States of Texas was the last real authority able to move freely on the continent. They had the strength of the military backing them and, with the use of their bands of Texas Rangers, were becoming famous across the badlands. However, not all of their exploits were popular; especially when it came to the robbing of supply convoys headed to the Midwest Alliance. There were rumors of full-on skirmishes along border areas and destruction of remote outposts. The Republic was lost. What remained was crumbling, and nobody thought Texas could do anything about it.

"Texas Rangers," Brad sighed and looked down at his calloused hands. "I ain't interested."

"They want our help getting in contact with the Midwest Alliance; they want to start peace talks." Brooks looked across the table. "I wouldn't come all the way out here if it wasn't important. Sean is already putting a team together; they will be here this evening. We'd like you to join us."

Brad pursed his lips and looked away. "You wasted your time looking for me; I won't fight for them, and I sure as hell won't kill for them. I am done with that, Brooks. How many have we killed already?"

Brooks grinned. "We're still here, aren't we?"

"What good has it done? The Primals are still out there, and now we're killing each other out on the frontier. And for what? Territory and canned vegetables."

Brooks shrugged and took another sip from the jar. "It could get you home. Back to Michigan. That is where you were headed, right? Just guides, Bro, walk in the park. Hell, Texas is the only one serious about putting this country back together again. Maybe we can make this work."

"Talks? Like the talks they had with the C.N.R.T?" Brad said. "Like the ones you and Sean had in that mountain?"

Brooks dipped his chin and frowned. "They had to be stopped. You knew what they were up to; you were there."

Brad looked down at his rucksack. "You were right about the pack. I'm leaving."

"You should wait until spring; winter isn't a good time to be out there all alone."

He grimaced, knowing his friend was right. "If I don't go now, I might never. Besides, the Primals will be slower in the winter. More predictable." He bluffed.

"When you leaving then? Sean will be here soon; I'm sure he'd like to see you off."

Brad smiled, knowing that the old SEAL chief would really try to talk him out of leaving, and would most likely succeed. If he was going to ever get home to Northern Michigan, then today was the day. He lifted the jar and finished the last of the whiskey, feeling the burn as it flowed into his belly. "Was good seeing you, Brooks. I'm sorry you wasted your time."

Chapter 2

**Two miles south of The Outpost,
Free Virginia Territories.**

Blowing snow cut the trail. It was bitterly cold and miserable; every step reminded the men that a storm was moving over the top of the mountain. Sean stepped ahead of the other men and lowered his scarf, looking down the narrow path that dropped along the mountain's face.

Looking behind him, he saw the two Texas Rangers. The men were covered in heavy oilskin jackets, wool scarves wrapped around their necks. His own men made up the rest of the small patrol. Sean stood watching as the soldiers slowly made their way up the trail.

"Problem, Chief?" a Ranger asked. Burt — a tall, wiry man — he was the leader and the older of the two Texans. Affable enough as far as Sean could tell, and he was not pushy, which was a good trait when asking for help these days.

"Bad weather coming in." Sean said, nearly shouting over the wind.

"It going to be a problem for us?" Burt asked.

Sean shook his head no. "The Outpost isn't much farther, we can rest up there," he said. He waited for the last of his men to move into sight, then turned back and continued up the trail. His vision was fading with the intensity of the storm. Gray sky blanketed by the thick, cottony clouds blew horizontal to his front. He opened his mouth and felt the cold sting against his tongue.

He looked at the ground; the trail had already dusted over, blocking the gravel surface ahead. Soon they would be trudging in deep snow. He stopped again, listening to the breathing of the men on the trail behind him. Instinctively, his eyes wandered up to the slope to the heavy, brush-laden tree lines above him. The trail was on the slanting edge of a ridge. At the top was a thick line of dark trees; below was nothing but jagged shale and rock.

Something felt off about the place. Sean reached to his chest and checked the heavy scoped rifle clipped to his vest. He kept his eyes on the trees, the feeling of being watched suddenly coming over him. It was a sense, something most men have but only the best of men are able to detect. A tingle or a rising of the hairs on the back of his neck; Sean had felt it before, moments before contact with an enemy or the explosion of a roadside bomb.

Sean dove for cover in the same instant that he felt the disruption of a round zipping through the air. He landed hard on the uphill side of the trail, crawling for the cover of large boulders. Pulling his body in tight, he tried to disappear within the snow covered rocks. The crack of the sniper's single shot echoed off the heavy cloud cover. He looked back and could see his men scrambling to both sides of the trail. Behind him, he saw the body of the young Ranger. The man's mouth was gaping open, a cloud of condensation seeming to hang over the dead man's lips, a perfectly round hole punched just over the Ranger's right eye. Blood seeped from behind the man's head, painting the freshly fallen snow bright red.

Sean locked eyes with Burt, who had tucked into the rocks beside the body of the fallen Ranger. "Is he alive?" Burt asked without lifting his head to look.

Sean shook his head no.

"Do you see the shooter?"

Grimacing, Sean exhaled and pressed back against the rock. Slowly, he raised his head so that he could see over the edge of the large boulder pile. He scanned the tree line, searching the tall, dark pine trees for any sign of the attacker. Finding nothing, he dropped back down and looked at Burt, shaking his head. "I don't see anything."

Laying against the snow-covered ground, he suddenly felt the cold seep into his clothing. The sweat at the center of his back was beginning to cool. They could not stay in the rocks forever; soon, they would have to move. Sean looked back at his men and gave them a hand signal to get on line and prepare to move up the slope toward the trees. It was a risky move against a hidden shooter; they would be smart to wait until dark and try to pull back. Sean looked up at the falling snow. They would freeze before they escaped, and who knows if the shooter had night vision. He grimaced hard and looked back at his men, nodding for them to advance.

Sean would not ask his men to expose themselves to the sniper alone, so he was the first to break cover. Moving out of the boulder pile with his rifle up and at the ready, he expected a shot to come at any moment. He climbed beyond the trail and into vegetation. Stopping, he took a knee, now scanning the far off trees through the scope of his own rifle. He looked left and could see the rest of his men cautiously moving from cover and climbing the slope. Burt crept forward and knelt beside him.

The veteran SEAL felt exposed and naked, kneeling in the high grass using his own men as bait while they advanced up the slope. His heart raced as he waited for the next bullet to rip through his own skull. With his men on line, he waved them on and covered their advance through the scope of his rifle. He clenched his teeth, knowing he would only have a split second; he hoped it was a single shooter.

The Ranger moved in closer. "Why haven't they shot again?"

"Shut up and spot for me," Sean scorned. "Watch for movement in those trees."

Sean leaned in, panning with the scope. He had not seen the muzzle flash, and the report of the rifle came long after the zip of the round. The shooter had to be far away. His eye locked on a downed tree. Snow lay in a straight bank along the logs surface, but part of the clean edge was knocked away and pressed down at the center. As his brain registered what he was looking at, he watched a man cloaked in a gray overcoat rise up from behind the log and extend his rifle.

Sean fired first, hurrying to get off the shot before the enemy sniper could target his men exposed on the slope. His round went low and to the right, kicking up a flash of cold powder and tree bark. The sniper flinched and pivoted. He locked onto Sean's position; instead of returning to cover, he tried to aim his rifle. It was a fatal mistake. Sean pulled the trigger a second time, launching a .308 round from his AR10 at over three thousand feet per second. The sniper's head snapped back and splash of blood sprayed the pristine white snow surrounding the sniper's hide.

"You got him!" Burt shouted.

"Keep looking, there might be another."

Sean kept his eye to the glass, searching. The downed man did not move. He scanned all along the ridge covering the approach as the first of his men reached the sniper's hole. He looked up into the face of his Pashto scout. The man carried an AK47 at the low ready and moved expertly over the rough face of the rocky slope. He knelt down then turned back to Sean. Hassan held his hand in the air and waved it in a circle.

Sean nodded and got to his feet. He turned back to see Burt going over the fallen Ranger's clothing. "Something you want to tell me?"

Burt kept his eyes on the task, reaching down to remove the gun belt from the dead man. "This is your territory; I thought you said it was safe out here."

"It is safe," Sean, rebutted.

"Tell that to my man," Burt said. He finished removing the dead man's valuables and wrapped the heavy trench coat around the body. "You get a lot of bandits out here?" He rolled the body and removed a black leather pack from the man's back.

"Bandits?" Sean grunted. "That was an assassin, and he was after your man."

Burt stood and wiped blood from his hands onto the outside of his coat. He shook his head and looked at the patrol now positioned around the sniper's den in a tactical stance. "We should join the others; might not be safe in the open here." He prepared to step off when Sean grabbed him by the shoulder.

"You need to tell me what's going on before we get up there."

The ranger pulled away. "I told you, it was a bandit."

"Bandits rob the weak... that man was lying up there in wait. He avoided all these easy targets and took down your man, and then he hung around. Probably to get a second shot at you," Sean said. "You need to tell me who the hell it was, or were turning back."

"Texas is paying your group a lot of food and ammo for this trip."

"You are paying us to guide you through Primal territory to the Midwest lines; not to get our asses picked off by snipers."

Burt nodded and looked up the slope then back at Sean. He held up the pack and said, "There is a bounty on this. I had no idea that word of its location would've reached this far."

"What is it?"

"Get us somewhere safe and I'll explain."

Sean ignored the demand and turned to move up the slope. At the top, he found his men gathered around the sniper. A scoped Remington Model 700 was leaning against the blood-spattered log. The man wore a gray and white tiger-striped overcoat; beneath it he wore tactical clothing—light blue fatigues with a gray, digital block pattern scattered over it. Joey

Villages, the group's Marine rifleman, already had the body's pockets turned out. He turned and looked up as Sean approached.

"What do you got?" Sean asked.

"Chief, this guy isn't no Cholo. Looks like a pro to me. His rifle is clean, he's wearing no patches, no identification, but he's packing a GPS."

Sean pursed his lips, and reached out a hand. "GPS? All the birds went down months ago."

Joey nodded. "I know, right? But look at this thing; it's still humming," he said, handing the small green device off to Sean. "Look — it's got way points all pre-loaded. This guy knows where all our shit is at: Camp Cloud, the outpost, even some of our safe houses. And there's more; these tracks? I'd say his spotter bugged out. I sent Sergeant Cole and a couple others to scout ahead."

Sean dipped his chin and flipped through the screen of the GPS, cycling right and recognizing the stored destinations. He turned and tossed the device to Burt. He stepped toward the fleeing man's boot prints in the snow. Looking up at Burt, he said, "You going to tell me what the hell is going on here?"

Burt looked at the men surrounding him uneasily. "Look, I just lost a Ranger; I'm as eager to know who this is as the rest of you are."

"Bullshit," Sean said, closing the distance between them. "Shine some light on it, or I'm pulling out."

The Ranger shook his head. "There is no pulling out now; they know who you are, where you live, and where you sleep. You're in it just as deep as Texas is now."

Chapter 3

The Outpost,
Free Virginia Territories.

"Sure you won't change your mind?" Brooks asked him.

The two men walked toward a high wall of vertically placed logs on the north side of the outpost, the tops of the logs sharpened to fine tips then buried in the ground side by side. Along the top of the wall was a narrow catwalk that the outpost's residents used in case of attack. Comprised of few buildings — less than a half dozen in total — the entire compound was effectively surrounded by the wall. Aside from the tavern, there was a pair of bunkhouses, a mess hall, and an old barn that they used for storage.

Brad adjusted the ruck on his back and pulled a shoulder strap tight. Snow was dropping in wet, heavy flakes. He could feel the chill on his face, but the whiskey still gave him a sense of courage to put the place behind him. He looked ahead to a guard staffing the gate, who then nodded to Brad and slid back a long plank that allowed the gate to swing open. Brad stopped and turned back to his friend. "I've got to do this. I've been putting it off for too long now as it is."

"I'll go with you; just ask," Brooks said. "The wilderness isn't a good place to be alone."

Brad shook his head. "No. Sean sent you up here to get me. I know he would be more than pissed if you ended up joining me instead."

"The Midwest is a wreck, Brad. I know you've heard the same stories I have… the food riots, mass killings. I really think you should reconsider."

Brad remained silent, and Brooks knew he would not convince him to stay, so the big man just clenched his jaw and nodded. Brooks extended his hand and the two men shook. "Good luck to you, Brad. I hope you find what you're looking for."

He forced a smile and turned away, then headed for the open gate and the road beyond it. Brad had to force every footstep, wanting to turn back but knowing he needed to get home to find his family, or at least know what happened to them. He made a silent promise to return to this place one day, but knew in his heart that he never would.

Passing beyond the gates onto the snow-covered path, he looked far into the distance of endless rows of pine trees and the purple sky behind it. He followed the two-trek road in a trance, letting the after-effects of the whiskey take his thoughts. He knew it was a bad idea to travel this way groggy and unaware. Brad reached down, grabbed a handful of snow, and pressed it to his neck, letting it shock him back to his senses.

He was moving along an old, mountain logging trail. Grass and weeds now covered most of the surface, as it had been well over two years since the last vehicle had traveled there.

Brad did not have much of a map; not one that would do him any good in the back country, anyhow. Just an old, county road guide and a military issue compass. Both sides of the road were flanked by uncut forest. Whichever logging company once worked there, for whatever reason, never got around to clearing that bit of the mountain; and now they never would.

From early planning and speaking with a couple of the locals, he knew the road would lead him out of the pass and onto a main highway. From there, he planned to continue north, moving out of the mountains and along the old interstates. Maybe find a small town and, hopefully, a truck. All of this while avoiding the Primals and, even worse, the others that wandered the back woods these days. Brad walked until the road curved and banked around, still moving out of the mountains. Several times, he saw the opening of trailheads and game trails.

He knew that the woods could be full of Primals the farther he got from the outpost, especially down in the lowlands and in the towns. For the time being, he would stick to the main roads and on the easier to travel terrain. The weather continued to worsen, the snow falling swiftly and the winds blowing in hard from the west. Brad did not mind; after two years of surviving the Primal holocaust, he knew the creatures did not like to venture out in foul weather. They tended to stay in whatever hives or nest they hid in when they weather got rough. He preferred a battle with Mother Nature over one with a pack of hungry Primals.

Brad's plan was to make it to a small hunter's cabin less than eight miles away before dark. He could rest up there, take in food and water, then leave again at first light. He had been to the place several times in the past year. It was nothing more than a box with a roof, but it would give him a place to stay the night, and it was on the approach to a small town at the bottom of the valley. There, he hoped to gain some sort of transportation to speed up his travel. As Brad moved, he scanned the surrounding terrain. He felt safe from the Primals still high on the mountain and in the heavy snowfall, but it never paid to take chances out in the bush.

The Primals had changed over the last two years. What started as crazy, rage-filled monsters had slowly become something else. Now they were more like wolves or lions — fierce pack hunters. They were smarter than humans had originally thought they were. As the virus set in, the stronger of them seemed to evolve; now they survived in packs, hunting and living in small family units. For the most part, they now stayed away from built-up camps, the same way a wolf or any other predator would have stayed away from a city before the fall. The Primals were smart and learned what uninfected humans could do to them.

Even with that, they were still dangerous on their own turf. And there, deep in the wilderness, was their hunting grounds. Brad had encountered them several times in the last month. Usually, he was high in a tree, hunting deer for the camp's stoves. He would see them moving along a game trail in small groups, stalking prey of their own. The creatures moved slowly, prowling through the forest like man-sized Sasquatches. They were now part of the food chain, APEX predators hunting the same game that Brad hunted.

After hours of marching at an intense pace, he came to the bend in the road. The logging trail made a sharp turn and angled steeply down. You would not know there was a place just above the corner without leaving the trail. At the sharp corner, Brad found a downed pine tree and followed it to a steep embankment. Trees and the slope of the terrain hid the small, one room cabin. Brad moved to the corner and stepped off the shoulder of the road and into the brush, then stopped and pivoted. Looking up through the haze of the falling snow, he could just see the outline of the cabin's gable roof.

Slowly, Brad readied his rifle and moved up the incline toward the small structure. Where bundles of thick vines and thorns ended, there was a building made of stacked square timbers. With the front porch of the small cabin partially collapsed, the front door was concealed under broken rafters. Brad cautiously circled around the building to a back door, a full heap of recently stacked firewood positioned just beside it. Brad moved to the door and stood listening. It would not be unusual for hunters to spend the night here. The last thing he wanted to do was startle an armed man on the inside.

Lightly, he wrapped his knuckles against the door. Once satisfied he was alone, he reached down and tried the door; it opened with a clunk in his gloved hand. He waited again for a moment to pass then stepped inside and quickly closed the door behind him. Keeping his rifle at the ready, he stood in the dark space, allowing his eyes to adjust to the low light. He could smell the smoky air, and the absence of the Primal stench let him know the place was safe.

The cabin was a twenty by twenty foot square, the floor made of flagstone and the walls of rough, scraped pine logs. A woodstove sat against one wall, a bed on the other, and a pair of chairs in the corner. Every window in the small cabin was shuttered and nailed shut. Brad turned behind him and placed a steel bar over the door to secure it. The place was a refuge in hostile grounds; well built. He had spent more than one night barricaded behind its walls. He knew when the sun went down, the Primals would come; they always did.

Brad was exhausted, alone, and cold. He dropped his pack and slid it against the door. On the wall were heavy, hooded sweatshirts and canvas coats hanging from wooden pegs. Brad slid off his own wet jacket and overshirts and swapped them for a dry sweatshirt. He moved across the space to the stove and built a small fire from pieces of dry wood. He removed his wet boots and socks and placed them in front of the fire to dry. A cabinet near the stove contained meager emergency rations for stranded travelers—a bag of rice, some dried meat, and a tin of crackers.

Brad left the rations where they were and removed a leather satchel from his pack. Inside the satchel were canned goods. He selected a tin of baked beans that he opened and placed on top of the stove. As the cabin warmed from the fire, he heard the first of their calls. The Primals were awake and on the hunt. They would most likely come to the cabin as they had before; they would smell the smoke and know it was occupied. They'd try the doors and look for a way in, but they wouldn't find a way past the heavy planks and boarded up windows. Before morning came, they would tire and move on. They always did.

Brad put his hand to the can of beans and removed it from the stove top, taking it to the bed with him. He ate half the contents before placing it on a small table. Brad loaded a bundle of wood into the wood stove and closed the door. He dropped to the bed, and placed an M9 on the nightstand, and a second sigma 9mm pistol under the pillow. He lay listening to the sounds of the Primals calling to each other, and closed his eyes to sleep.

As Brad's thoughts drifted, he heard a pounding at the door. A scraping of wood and the rattle of the lock. He let his hand drift to his sidearm resting at the edge of the bed. He turned up, watching the door. Even though he expected them, the Primals still scared him straight with every arrival. The door shuddered again and he heard a rapid knock.

"Come on, open the door. We can see the smoke from the chimney," a man's raspy voice whispered.

His back stiffened and his hand squeezed the grip of his pistol. He stared at the door.

"Come on, man, let us in," the voice called again.

Brad leaned forward. Transferring weight

to his feet, he stood and cautiously stepped to the door. He put his hand to the handle and raised his weapon. "Who are you?"

"Travelers, we come on this place. It was marked on our map. We got delayed, meant to get here before dark–" A loud Primal moan interrupted the man's words. "Please, open the door. They're getting closer."

Brad clenched his teeth and holstered his weapon. He unbarred the door and pulled it open, standing back as three men piled into the room. The last one in turned and quickly shoved the door closed behind him. Brad waited for the man to move, then re-barred the door, listening to the sounds of the Primals grow in intensity.

He moved away and returned to his seat near the bed. Brad kept his hand close to his weapon and looked the group over. Two were stocky, bearded men. Broad shouldered, they carried themselves like experienced woodsman. Behind them was a lanky man with scraggly facial hair. He did not seem to belong with the other two. The lanky man wore a gray, striped parka while the other two wore dark coats and canvas pants. The bearded men had hunting rifles; the lanky man had a semi automatic shotgun held loosely in his arms. Brad edged back and sat on the bed, watching the men peel off their jackets and move to the stove to warm themselves.

The oldest looking of the men turned to face him; his eyes were slits, his beard gray and covered with snow. "Sorry to barge in on ya like this. Hell, we know better than to get lost in the dark; guess we underestimated the distance. This your place then?"

"No, it's just a refuge," Brad said, watching the men closely.

"So, just you alone, then?"

Brad sat stoned-faced, not replying to the man's comments with anything other than a nod.

The man coughed and wiped his face with his sleeve. "Hell, where are my manners. I'm Bill Yeung; this here is Carl," the man said, pointing to the tall, shivering man who did not bother to look away from the fire. "And that's Gabe." The second bearded man looked at Brad and grimaced, then pointed to the open can of baked beans.

"You got any more of that grub," Gabe asked.

Brad nodded and pointed to the cabinet behind the man. "Some rice and jerky in there."

The man grinned, showing stained teeth, before he turned back and rummaged through the pantry.

"Sorry, friend, I didn't catch your name," Bill said, dropping down on a wooden chair near the stove to remove his boots.

"I didn't give it," Brad replied, still watching the men cautiously and noticing that all of them were still holding their rifles. Bill followed Brad's stare to the weapons.

"Ahh, nothing to be alarmed by," the man said, unslinging his rifle and leaning it in a corner. The other men looked at him then followed suit by placing their own weapons in the same spot. Brad relaxed his shoulders and exhaled.

"Name's Thompson, friends call me Brad," he said. "You said you had a map; where is it you're from?"

Bill furrowed his brow at the question. Brad watched as he exchanged glances with the other men, and then smiled. "Up north a ways from here, Hidden Springs; you heard of it?"

Brad shook his head no. "What are you doing down this way?"

"Headed to a settlement in the valley, a place they call Camp Cloud."

"I've heard of it. What business takes you there?"

"You know the place then?" Gabe asked, placing a cast iron pot filled with rice atop the stove. He began breaking off clumps of the jerky into it. "Is it far?"

"What takes you there?" Brad asked again, not answering the question.

Bill moved closer to the stove and Brad saw the lump at his waistline. The outline of a concealed weapon. The man removed a bottle of water from his pack and added it to the pot. "Meeting some folks," he said, causing Gage to shoot him a stern look. Bill raised his chin and turned to look directly at Brad. "Now, why don't you go ahead and clear your side arm for me."

Brad pressed back. From the corner of his eye, he saw that in his distraction, the tall man had managed to draw and aim a nickel-plated revolver at his chest. The lanky man looked frightened; Gabe stood with a wide smile breaking across his face just beside him. Brad slowly put his hands in the air.

A thump against the door let them all know that the Primals had surrounded the cabin and knew they were inside. The tall man's hand shook with the impacts of the creatures outside the door.

"Now, just relax, they can't get in here," Brad said. Showing his open palms, he turned his hip toward Bill, offering the holstered weapon. "You know I don't want any trouble from you gentleman; I'm just here to wait out the night, same as you. Come morning, I'll be on my way."

"Oh, there isn't going to be no trouble, I can assure you that," Bill said. Closing the distance, he removed the weapon from Brad's holster and walked across the room. He dropped it heavily on the small nightstand. Brad scooted so that he was on the center of the bed. He still had a knife at the center of his back, and he would use it if the men attempted to restrain him. He slowly lowered his hands and placed them on his thighs, then watched as Bill casually crossed the room and sat back in the chair.

"You could leave here alive, if you are kind enough to answer a few questions," Bill said.

The old man leaned back as the other bearded man handed him a large bowl of rice. Bill took a handful, pressing it between his lips, and looked up at Brad. "So, tell me what you know about the camp."

Brad sighed and stretched his arms so that they were behind him and away from the side table. He opened his fingers and rested his hands on the dingy mattress, propping him up. Without looking, he estimated the distance to the pillow where he knew his backup pistol lay concealed. "I wish it hadn't gone like this. When I saw you folks, I really had hopes that you were just travelers. So much talk of bandits and robbers these days. Just not enough good people out here anymore."

"Them's the breaks," Bill said, chuckling and stuffing another mouthful of rice into his mouth. "Now, tell me about the camp."

Brad looked down and flinched as a loud boom reverberated through the cabin. A thumping from above sent dust shaking from the rafters. As the men in the room looked up to hear the Primals on the roof, Brad dropped to his side. He retrieved the Sigma pistol and, with rehearsed motions, leveled his arm and locked onto the armed, lanky man. A single pull of the trigger and the tall man bucked back; his arms went limp, dropping the revolver.

The gunshot's blast compressed inside the tight space, causing Brad's ears to ring as he shifted his aim to the next man. Gabe looked at him in shock. He reached for a rifle, and Brad fired again, the round entering below the man's bearded jaw. Brad pressed back and again shifted his point of aim, looking down the sights into the wide eyes of Bill.

The gunfire agitated the Primals; he could

hear them scrambling on the roof, scraping against the cabin's log walls. Brad let the front sight rest on the man's chest. He was breathing heavily, in shock from the quick violence that just took his friends. The man looked at the bodies on the stone floor, and then turned back to Brad. "Why did you do this? We wouldn't have killed you."

"I didn't stay alive this long gambling," Brad said, getting to his feet. He walked to the downed men and checked the corpses. Bill glared at him, the shock turning to rage.

Brad kicked at the lanky man then turned to the other. "Sorry about your people, but you didn't give me a choice." After confirming both men were dead; he grabbed an empty chair and dragged it across the room, positioning it in front of Bill.

He rested his hand on his lap, still keeping the Sigma's barrel in the direction of the old man's chest. "So, what business do you have at Camp Cloud?"

The old man gritted his teeth and snarled. "I ought to kill ya," he said.

Brad shook his head. "You had your chance. Now, why Cloud?"

Bill's voice was quiet as he mumbled so Brad could not tell what he was saying; the words came out like a snarl. Brad let his hand caress the pistol grip. "What was that you said?"

"They'll kill you. They are going to kill all of you."

Brad bit down on his lower lip, his jaw stiffened. His hand shook as his eyes fixed on the man across from him. He wished he had brought a jar of the tavern whiskey with him on this trip, just enough to calm his nerves. Brad rolled his shoulders and looked back at the man. "Who?"

Bill shook his head. "You're as good as dead now. There will be no coming back from this. Maybe killing Gabe, even killing me; you still coulda walked from that. But killing the shithead over there? He won't let that slide."

Brad was losing his patience. He shifted forward and pressed the barrel of the pistol against the man's forehead. "Who the hell are you talking about?"

"General Carson, you fool. He's moving on everyone, he's taking everything, and he don't care who you are."

Brad lowered the gun and settled back. "Who is General Carson?"

Bill let out a sadistic laugh. "You *don't know* Carson?" The man laughed again. "Well, you just killed his damn son."

Brad looked to the lanky man. "Who? Stretch over there?"

"Stretch, ha. He's going to kill you. And if he finds me here alive after what you done, he'll go right back to Hidden Springs and kill mine and Gabe's family too."

"I don't understand," Brad said.

The bearded man let out a cruel laugh. "There isn't nothing to understand. Nothing you can do now. They will find you in the morning; they are out there right now, I bet! They'll kill you and everyone at Cloud too; he'll kill all of you," Bill shouted, spittle hitting Brad's face. The man lunged forward from his chair. The swift movement catching Brad off guard, the men collided and spilled to the stone floor.

Brad struggled to hold the gun; he twisted as the man rained punches down. Brad felt his nose break. He took blow after blow, telling himself to stay conscious. He grabbed the man's shirt with his free hand. Pulling the man in, he threw his knee into his side and gut repeatedly. Bill feigned back, and went for a knife strapped to his belt.

Brad grabbed the man's wrist, lurched up, and head butted him, dazing both men. Bill leaned back, letting go. He tried to climb to a knee as he released the knife from its sheath and stabbed down. Brad found the pistol and fired first. The rounds found Bill's chest, the bearded man's body going slack and collapsing down.

Chapter 4

Camp Cloud
Free Virginia Territories

Chelsea took a knee on the most westerly wall of the perimeter fence where it overlooked an expansive pasture that gently rolled down to the now frozen and snow covered lake. The fence was newly built out of old materials. In most places, it was little more than a few stacked logs; in others, an open trench. There was not much need for Primal protection at Camp Cloud in the heart of the Cloud's property. The homestead at the bottom of the valley and the outpost on the north side provided plenty. She normally did not stand watch, but with half the guard force out on patrol with Chief Rogers, she had volunteered.

The crunching of fresh snow from behind caused her to turn her head. She looked back to see Shane approaching with a steel thermos. His heavy shirt had the collar turned up. She smiled and reached out a hand, taking the container. "What are you doing awake?" she asked him. She removed the cap and used it as a mug, pouring in the venison broth.

Shane pointed at clear, black sky filled with bright stars. "Temperatures are dropping; I thought you could use something to warm you up." He moved past her and leaned against one of the large fence posts that supported the barrier. "I still don't know why we bother with a guard force. We've never seen one of them this far up the valley."

She smiled and took another swallow of the soup, then held the cup, letting the heat warm her hands. They had had the argument before, but it was part of their life now — it was the price for living in the free territories. She knew Shane would prefer to take Ella south to Texas, to live in the fortified safe areas — she also knew that Shane would never go without her.

Chelsea drained the last of the cup and

replaced the lid to the thermos. She moved closer and leaned against the fence, looking out over the snow-covered lake. She put a hand on his shoulder and he moved closer, sheltering her from the wind. "We should leave," he whispered. "Go south so we don't have to face the winters."

She held up a hand, silencing him. A flash of light in the far tree line caught her eye. She squinted and leaned in, trying to focus on the dark spaces beyond the lake. Without looking away, she reached for the binoculars hanging from her neck.

"What is it?" Shane asked.

"I don't know, I—" She gasped; several shadows moved through the trees, using them as cover to move around the lake. She pivoted to the left where the trees converged into the short field that separated itself from their perimeter fence. She just caught a glimpse of a man breaking cover and running through the tall grass. Pushing out and looking farther left, she saw more gathered around a distant observation tower. The guard was dead; his body hanging over the side. She then spotted the men that were climbing the walls.

"The alarm, Shane, sound the alarm!" she gasped again.

With fear in his eyes, he obeyed her order, reaching for the flare gun secured to the post by a length of nylon cord. He aimed it overhead and fired. A red starburst flare flew into the air and popped. The flares had a double effect, they would warn the other towers of an attack, and it would draw in nearby Primals to attack anything outside the protective walls. Moments after the flare, tracer rounds arced in from the tree lines and the camp exploded with gunfire. Chelsea ducked behind the log barrier then stood, leveling her rifle. She fired off an entire magazine into the source of the tracers.

Shane grabbed at her jacket, pulling her back into cover an instant before the logs shattered with the impact of return fire.

"We have to go! We have to go now!" Shane shouted. More rounds exploded into the wall, the camp filled with screams and gunfire, and the sky above them became painted with flares from all along the perimeter fence. Chelsea lurched back, falling into the snow, and looked at him; he had his pistol out, aimed somewhere beyond her, and fired three shots. She turned in time to see a man dressed in gray camouflage fall to the ground.

"We have to get to Ella," he screamed at her.

She nodded furiously and pushed him ahead of her, swapping magazines in her rifle as she followed. Turning, she spotted four men running in their direction; one stopped to fire. She raised her rifle and yelled for Shane to run. The scream caught the attacker's attention and the man turned his rifle in her direction and fired, the shot going high. She dove forward, the deep snow smacking into her face, then crawled ahead, pulling herself up to her elbows. Taking cover behind a wooden cart, she rose up and squeezed the trigger, hitting the shooter twice in the chest.

She saw Shane across the open space at the corner of a building. He was leaning out and firing at the approaching men. More had joined the fight and were returning fire; rounds smacked into the log walls and the hard-packed snow.

"Go get Ella!" she screamed at him, knowing she was pinned. Chelsea pivoted and focused on the new targets. Two men broke cover and ran forward. She pulled the trigger rapidly, watching the men spin out of control and crash to the ground.

Rounds impacted deep in the snow all around her. She looked back to the front and saw a gunman closing on her; she pivoted back and fired blind, watching the point blank shot enter just below the nose and exit through the back of his brain. The whistling of mortar fire and a blinding explosion from the left turned her away. The ground around her exploded with gunfire. She refused to back off, holding her position, firing and changing magazines as the men closed in on the camp's buildings.

A blast in her chest knocked her back. She felt the warmth of blood leaving her body. Her legs grew numb; she rolled to her side in an attempt to reload her rifle. Coughing blood, she winced at the white-hot pain from her broken ribs. She collapsed to the ground, struggling to turn her head. She saw the building where

Shane had stood; it was in flames, and he was gone. She fell back, too tired to move as men in gray parkas ran past her, ignoring the bleeding body on the ground.

Chapter 5

**The Outpost,
Free Virginia Territories**

"What's with this guy?" Brooks asked.

The Ranger sat beside Sean at the table; the Texan used a bowie knife to slice through the slab of rare meat on his plate. He stuffed a chunk into his mouth and chewed. They were in a large mess building in the center of the outpost. The men of the patrol gathered inside, sitting at tables around a large communal fireplace. A slab of wild boar was roasting over the flames as a cook sliced chunks from the carcass.

Sean reached across the table for a pitcher of water and filled a drinking glass before pushing it toward Burt. "Okay, this is about as safe as it gets. Now tell me what this is all about."

Burt chewed then reached for the glass

and drank thirstily, placing the empty back on the table. The man looked left and right and could see that the others in the room were preoccupied with their own meals. "Okay, but I have to warn you, I was sworn to keep these secrets. You won't like the truth."

Brooks stabbed his own knife into the tabletop. "Just spit it out. This is more than a routine patrol to the North."

The Ranger clenched his jaw and nodded. He was playing his cards close and it was visibly agitating Sean. "We are on the brink of war— well, judging by what happened today, we may already be at war," Burt said.

"The hell are you talking about?" Sean asked, refilling the water glass.

The Ranger dropped his knife and pushed the dinner plate away. He exhaled loudly and again let his eyes sweep the room. He dug through a shirt pocket and pulled out a cigar; he stuck it in the corner of his mouth, leaving it unlit. "Tell me, Chief, what do you know about what's happening in the cities up north?"

Sean scowled; he looked over at Brooks then back at the Ranger. "We've had refugees pass through on the route to Texas. Hungry, tired — they don't say much; just that they are looking for something better. It's been months since the last one though."

Nodding, the Ranger wiped his chin and used a match to light the cigar. "I think you've heard more than that, but don't want to hear it. The North is falling apart, Chief. The government's collapsed, people are starving." The Ranger paused, allowing Sean to digest his response.

"What do you mean the government's collapsed?" Sean asked.

Burt smiled. "You really haven't heard; I thought you were just messing with me." He laughed. "You all really are out here in the dark! Damn, Chief — New Philadelphia is gone; the governor's council is all dead. The Alliance is breaking."

Sean looked up at the mess hall's rafters as though he were studying a complex problem in his head. He rubbed the stubble on his chin with the back of his hand and said, "If this is true, why the hell didn't you tell us before asking for a guide to take you north?"

Burt slid back in his seat and crossed his hands on the table in front of him. He looked at Sean, considering his reply before he spoke. "Because we knew you'd refuse if we came out and said it. It's you all's fault really. Dan Cloud and his damn efforts to stay neutral."

"So this trip north, it's all a charade? If it wasn't to barter for peace, then what's it really about?" Brooks interrupted.

The Ranger leaned forward; he was beginning to show annoyance at being so thoroughly questioned. "Listen, the peace mission is real enough; it's just more complicated than that. The Midwest Alliance has split in half. Not really split, I guess, more like *been reduced*. Shit like that happens when you run out of food and resources."

Brooks squinted and leaned in. "So, if the governor's council is gone, who were we going to meet?"

"That's the thing, boys; the entire

government isn't *gone*. Like I said, it's reduced. We still have the strongholds in Michigan looking for help, begging for our protection."

Sean raised a hand. "Help? Protection? From who?" he asked.

Burt removed the leather satchel from the pack at his feet and placed it on the table to his front. "He calls himself General Carson. He is not on our books; no pre-war records of him. Best we can figure, he was a member of one of the militia groups," Burt said. "He's managed to organize a large group, taking over small camps like this one as he moves east toward Michigan lines. He's running a scorched earth campaign, sending everything he takes back to New Philadelphia — or what he now calls Carsonville."

Sean was still pondering the problem, but began to show the realization of the situation they were in. It was not their first time being used, or trapped between warring groups. "Back there on the mountain, you said we were in it now; what the hell does any of this have to do with us?" Sean asked.

Burt flipped open the satchel and removed a stack of papers. "The MWA has agreed to join Texas. This is the signed treaty. This makes it official; it puts us at war with Carson."

Brooks scoffed. "What the hell does a treaty like that matter out here?"

"I get that it's symbolic, but it matters to the people." Burt took in a deep breath. "Just them knowing we're still something more than a third world shantytown helps keep them going, and stops them from surrendering to this asshole. This agreement is a start to rebuilding the Republic. It's more than peace; it's a new start."

"Nothing like a new enemy to bring people together." Sean shrugged. "Guess it makes no difference now because we're not going anywhere until we talk to the colonel. You've misled us."

The Ranger's eyes glimmered in the low light. "Like I said, you're in it now. Without Texas, you won't be able to stand against them; they'll be after your things."

Brooks grunted again. "What things?"

"Based on reports, everything you got. Carson is no gentleman. He will kill off every man you have, take every woman and child. He will take your food, your weapons, and your territory. Any man that he decides to let live will be forced to join his ranks."

"You know, you should have led with that," Sean said.

"I'm sorry, but we couldn't let anyone know we were transporting the signed treaty."

"Well, secret's out," Sean said. "So, this Carson… what makes you think he'll come after us?"

The Ranger nodded, his face suddenly turning hard. "Carson wants to stop the Midwest from joining Texas; he wants to keep our military and the Rangers out of his little Civil War he's got going. They hit us on the trail to try to intercept the treaty. However, from the looks of the GPS, they have been here for a while. I'm sorry, but none of your people are safe. You won't be able to stay out of this fight."

The door flew open and a stocky man barged into the room. A panicked voice echoed.

"Is that Joe-Mac?" Brooks asked. "What the hell is he doing here?"

The young man locked eyes on the group at the table and ran through the crowd. Sean and Brooks looked up at Joe-Mac, who rested his shaking hands on the table, leaning hard to stay upright. His eyes were blood shot, his clothing stained with mud.

"Hell, son, I thought you were down at Camp Cloud," Sean said.

Joe-Mac nodded, gulping in air. "I was, Chief. I came as quick as I could." A series of gunshots echoed from outside. Joe-Mac turned to look behind him. "It's okay; some Primals followed me up, but the guards can handle it."

"You traveled in the dark?" Brooks asked.

Joe-Mac nodded again. "Dan sent me, I took my truck—listen, Chief, the camp's been attacked," he gasped.

Brooks stood up and faced the young man, then asked the question he already knew the answer to. "Was it Primals?"

Joe-Mac did not immediately respond; he lowered his head, then looked back up. "No, sir, it was raiders. Everyone is dead or gone."

Sean stood, his arms and legs suddenly weak. The blood drained from his face as he walked to the young man and put a hand on his shoulder. "Slow down and tell me what happened."

"That's the thing, Chief; we don't know. Our lookouts saw the flares from the main house. The flare, that's how we knew it had to be Raiders; we never use flares during a Primal attack — that just makes it worse. Dan got every available man organized and sent us out. We took the trucks and went straight there, but — "

"But what?" Brooks asked.

"It's gone, Chief. They killed all the men, took the women and children. Stole all the stores, burned the buildings."

Burt stood and stuffed the leather satchel back into his pack. "That's Carson. He takes hostages, and sends them back east to repopulate his cites. Were your people vaccinated?" he asked.

Sean remained silent, still processing the information, his fists balled as he nodded his response.

"That will make them even more valuable to a man like Carson," Burt said.

Sean snarled and spun toward Burt; the men faced each other, only inches apart. "You knew this would happen and you didn't warn us."

"No, that's not it at all," Burt paused looking down at the table. After he collected his thoughts, he looked back up at Sean. "The papers can wait. Let's get your people back."

Sean grabbed his rifle that was leaning against the table. When he surveyed the room, he could see that his men had drawn in close and heard everything. Sean knew the men in the group had families in the camp. "We'll get them back. You can count on that."

Chapter 6

Lying on the stone floor, the man's body atop him, Brad woke to the sound of the Primals. He squirmed and rolled the corpse to the side, then pulled himself away. He reached up and felt the throbbing lump on the front of his head. He felt his face; his nose was crusted with blood, but not broken as he'd initially thought. The room was cold and dark, the fire in the stove had gone out. He pulled himself into a seated position and searched his pockets for his lighter; flicking the flint wheel, it ignited and lit the space.

The flames reflected off the glazed eyes of the bearded dead man. Brad shook his head slowly and crawled over the body. Opening the stove, he stirred the coals and added fuel to the fire. Soon it was again blazing bright and illuminating the interior of the cabin.

He searched the bodies and dumped the contents of their pockets. Placing them on the table, he carefully sorted through the objects. It was mostly garbage, aside from a wedding ring and a scrap of folded paper. Brad chucked the ring into the fire and unfolded the paper. It was an intricately drawn map of trails and geographic references, but most alarming was that it had the precise location of The Outpost, Camp Cloud, and the main house. When Brad turned the page over, he found a detailed drawing of Camp Cloud, identifying ranges and the tower locations, even the number of guards that would be on duty.

"Fuck," Brad whispered. "He was telling the truth."

Brad folded the paper and stuffed it in his breast pocket. He rummaged through the men's packs and transferred all of their ammo to his own. He took the tall man's shotgun and a half box of buckshot shells from his shirt pocket. He sat the weapon aside and moved back to his pack. Inside, he had a pair of night vision goggles; they were beat up and worn, but still serviceable. He removed them from the black carrying case and inserted his last set of batteries. Placing them on his head, he panned the room, then lifted them so that they rested above his eyes.

The Primals still howled and scratched at the door. They were agitated and looking for the food that they knew was inside. Brad looked past the bodies on the floor and thought of the map in his pocket. If the dead man had been telling the truth, Carson's men would be somewhere close; there were only a few other safe houses nearby, and an old livestock barn three miles up the road would be the most likely. As much as Brad would like to travel to the barn, he knew had to warn the Outpost.

He opened his pack and dumped the contents onto the bed. Forced to travel at night, he would have to be moving fast, so he needed to lighten the load. Brad removed the canned goods and his normal camping kit, leaving only ammo and water. Unzipping a front pouch, he removed two suppressors and attached one each to his M4 and M9. He put the Sigma in the rucksack and secured the straps. There was another series of bangs at the door, reminding him that he still had to contend with the Primals before he would be going anywhere.

Brad went back and retrieved the shotgun. A Remington 1100 with the barrel chopped. Brad unloaded it then reloaded, counting the five rounds going into the extended tube before he put the rest in his shirt pocket. He verified one in the pipe, then put on his pack and stood by the door. He clipped the M4 to his chest and used the shotgun stock to bang on the door. He wanted them all out front when he opened it.

He moved back to the stove and opened the cast iron door. Using a poker, he dumped hot coals to the floor then kicked them to the stacked firewood. He dumped the contents of the kindling box and watched as the dried material caught fire and quickly spread to the log walls. He hated to destroy the place, but he needed the fire to distract the Primals if he was going to get back to the Outpost. Brad grabbed bedding and added it to the flames.

"Cabins can be rebuilt; I can't," he said, turning away.

With the fire blazing behind him and the cabin filling with smoke, he moved toward the door that was now shuddering with the impact of Primals. Brad leveled the shotgun and aimed toward the top section that he knew once held a window and was made up of thinner wood. He fired three times. The first round having little effect, the second creating a hole, and the third destroying a Primal face that dared look inside. He stuck the barrel through the hole and fired until the tube was empty then quickly reloaded from the shells stuffed into his jacket pocket.

Not hearing more of the creatures, he kicked the door outward, scrambling quickly away from the door so that the burning fire would not silhouette him. Looking down at the shattered bodies, he heard the crunching behind him and spun, looking up as two of the things leapt down from the roof. He fired on the move, hitting one in the gut, the close range nearly ripping the creature in half. The second fell, crippled from the stray buckshot pellets. Brad heard their crying and the crashing of brush as more charged through the forest. He sidestepped to the corner of the cabin; the fire, now burning bright, spilled into the trees and exposed the mad faces of the Primals as they advanced.

Brad took aim and leaned into the shotgun, once again emptying it into the charging mass, creating maximum noise and chaos, before tossing it to his front. He slipped back into the shadow, readying his suppressed M4, and duck-walked along the perimeter of the cabin before dropping into the rough vegetation that led back toward the road. As he dropped his goggles over his eyes, he could hear the enraged creatures behind him falling for the distraction. Attracted to the noise and flames of the fire, they feverishly attacked the cabin.

He heard their screams and knew they were feasting on the dead inside. To the Primals, they were fresh meat and free for the taking. Brad pushed the thoughts aside as he moved down the incline and back to the surface of the road, then dropped into a gully and sat silently with his weapon held close to his chest. He pulled the goggles from his face and let his eyes adjust to the moonlight; snow was falling hard, causing the white surface of the road to glow, showing him the way. Brad brought the rifle up to his shoulder and cautiously checked his surroundings. The only noise came from up the hill behind him; the front appeared clear. He was sure that any of them in the vicinity would have been attracted to the virtual dinner bell in the cabin, with the tower of flame that rose up in the sky behind him.

Brad turned and pressed hard down the road. Walking the center, he knew they would more easily see him, but wanted the early warning if they made an attack. He started out slowly at first, then increased his pace to a jog. The pack bounced and rubbed against his back and the boots burned against the soles of his feet. It was eight miles to the outpost; he'd run farther on good days, but he knew this was not one of them.

Brooks was right about him. He had spent the last few months at the outpost mostly sulking; wasting his days either in the tavern or out on the trails hunting for game. Life at the outpost was about little more than survival, and he had lost his taste for it. He hoped he might find a brighter future back in Michigan, but after hearing rumors from travelers and hunters in the tavern, his gut told him things would be even worse at home. Brad put his hopes aside and went through the day trying to be optimistic that there was something better for him out there. He put off the trip home because he knew there was not.

After jogging and battling with his thoughts for over an hour, he slowed to a walk. His clothing now soaked with sweat, he was breathing hard, and clouds of condensation formed with every breath. The outpost was just ahead; he stopped and knelt down on the road to drink from his canteen while he listened for movement. The road was silent, the burning cabin now miles behind him; but ahead, he could hear gunfire coming from the outpost.

"No!" he shouted. "They can't be here already."

He forced himself back to his already sore feet and pushed off. He pushed on through the fresh snow, his legs heavy and calves cramping; he trudged ahead, forcing every step. The sounds of the gunfire and Primal moans led the way over his heavy breathing and burning lungs. As he approached the final hill, he could see the glow of the outpost's perimeter fence and the muzzle flashes of the guard's rifles. Brad stopped to pull down his NVGs and spotted movement in his peripheral vision.

Hunched shadows darted through the trees to his left and right. Suddenly, a pair would break and run directly at the fences, attempting scale the log wall, forcing the guards at the top to scramble to cut them down. Brad heard a rumbling through the tree line and the crashing of brush. He pivoted and took a knee, bringing up his rifle. A pack of five were running at a sprint, howling as they advanced, their heads turned and focused on the outpost — they did not see Brad tucked into the shadows.

He held his breath and raised the rifle, trying to estimate the sites through his night vision goggles. He let them get close then rapidly pulled the trigger, sweeping his point of aim as the Primals advanced. The muzzle blast washed out his night vision, the smoke from his rifle hanging heavy in the cold air. With his final shot, the screams stopped. Brad pushed forward and stood, a spotlight hit him and he raised his hands and turned toward the gate. A man in the tower cried out a challenge.

"It's me, Sergeant Thompson."

"Well, get your ass in here!" a man shouted back.

Brad kept his hands in the air and ran for the gate. He could hear the log bracing removed from the gate. He reached the opening and turned around; facing out into the darkness, he dropped the magazine on his M4 and replaced it with a full one. The gate pressed open, an arm grabbed his sleeve and pulled him inside. As the gate shut behind him, he stumbled forward, the feeling of safety turning his legs to jelly. He took an awkward step and stumbled, but Sean was there to grab him. He steadied Brad, helping him gain his balance.

Sean shook him and spoke into his ear, "You okay? Are you hurt?"

Brad looked down then back up again. "I'm fine." He reached into his pocket and handed Sean the map. "We have to get to Camp Cloud; they're all in danger," Brad said, his voice a whisper.

Sean pursed his lips and nodded. "I know, brother, just rest."

"We need to go before it's too late," Brad gasped.

Sean slung Brad's left arm over his shoulder and turned to walk him toward the bunkhouse. Brad saw the men from the camp gathered in front of the building. He tugged away from Sean and grabbed his shirt. "It's already happened, hasn't it?" he snapped.

The SEAL chief grimaced and dipped his chin. "Get some rest, Brad, we move out at first light."

"No, we have to go now," Brad said, trying to stand on his own, the day's march and the return run having taken a hard toll on his body.

Sean turned him away and walked him to the bunkhouse. "You need rest; we all do. We've been on the march all day; I can't turn them around now in this storm."

Brad pushed away. "I can walk on my own." He stopped and looked at the weary men.

Their heads were down, their boots and clothing still soaked from marching in the snow. Brad nodded his head and walked away toward the barracks.

Chapter 7

Free Virginia Territories

Shane awoke feeling peaceful and warm between soft sheets. He wiggled his toes, but when he went to stretch his arms, he felt the searing pain in his shoulder. Reaching instinctively, he felt the gauze and bandages. He then noticed he was in cotton boxers — not visually though; the space was black as coal and he could not see a hand in front of his face.

"Where am I? Is this heaven, or hell?"

The last thing he remembered was being in the forest, tracking the raiding party. He was attacked. The Primals. He put a hand back to his shoulder. "But they killed me," he whispered, recalling being wounded and laying in the brush with the dead creature pinning him to the ground, and blood seeping from his wound. He turned again and felt the pain from the shoulder wound. "So I'm alive, but where am I?"

He squinted and could barely make out the outline of a window covered in heavy drapes, the window itself probably covered in heavy shutters. Or maybe he was on a second floor. No way was it just glass; the Primals would have broken in ages ago if the room was unsecured. He held his breath and listened; nothing. The room was silent. In fact, the entire house was silent, not even a creak. Moving again, he noticed a plastic IV line going into his arm. He felt the end and followed it to a bag hanging over his head.

"Was I captured? Do the raiders have me?

"No, that's stupid; they would have killed me.

"Chief Rogers then; they found me. But why is the room so damn quiet? Where is everyone?"

Shane lay back and blinked his eyes, trying to make out the room in the darkness. He was not drugged; there was no loss of pain in his body. The room was warm; a fire must be going somewhere inside, and someone had to be close by tending to it.

He heard the slam of a door and heavy boots stomping somewhere below him, followed by the scuffing of furniture. The sounds were far away, but definitely below him; he was on a second floor. The only two-story home in the area was the Cloud main house, and he knew he was not there. There would be no reason to cover the window at the Cloud home. He heard a floorboard squeak and feet walking up stairs. The footfalls were growing closer. Shane lay back and closed his eyes, not ready to meet whomever had brought him here.

There was a rattle of floorboards, a clunking of a lock, and then the squeak of the door opening. A soft glow hit his closed eyelids. The boots echoed now that they were in the room. He heard the sounds of china placed on a table, then recognized the smell of stew.

"I know you ain't asleep," a gruff voice said.

Shane squeezed his hands, gripping the sheets, and opened his eyes.

An elderly man was standing over him. Short and stocky, he was dressed in a blue sweatshirt and wool cap. His face was leathery with deep crow's feet at the corners of his eyes. The man checked the IV and nodded before turning away. He moved across the small room and sat in a wooden chair. Shane pulled himself back and attempted to sit up. The man grinned then moved back toward Shane, who flinched. The man chuckled as he repositioned the pillows behind Shane's back.

"If'in I wanted ya hurt, I'da left you out in the woods."

"Why didn't you?" Shane said with a hoarse voice.

The old man grinned and poured Shane a glass of water from a stone pitcher. He reached out and Shane took the glass. Drinking quickly, he emptied it and passed the glass back. The old man refilled it and placed it next to the white china bowl.

"Curiosity, I guess. You looked good as dead when I found you. You have plenty of old wounds and scars, boy; you been around the block a few times. I seen the bite. That thing bit into you good, but I cut away your wound, and you ain't turned. No sign of the infection neither."

"I've been vaccinated," Shane said.

"Aye, I figured as much. I reckon you must be a soldier then; probably one of Gunny Cloud's boys down the mountain."

Shane nodded. "You know Dan?

"Yeah, I know Dan; he's good people. Heard he had a group livin' wit' him down there. I seen some of ya out huntin' on the mountain a time or two."

"Does he know you're here, mister…? I'm sorry, I don't know your name."

The old man smiled. "I reckon he does. We old guys are harder to kill than you might think. We traded house plans over pints back when he was building his homestead. My friends call me Henry, and I know your name is Shane."

"How?" he asked.

Henry smiled again and pointed to a laundry basket in the corner where Shane's clothes sat neatly folded inside. "It was sewn into the back of yer jacket."

Shane dipped his chin and eyed the stew. Henry caught his gaze and stood, helping the soldier take the bowl. He moved a tray table across his lap and again adjusted the pillows. Shane hungrily gulped away at the food, hardly breathing between bites.

"So, what were you doing out there? I saw the buck—what was left of it, anyway. It's a bit far for a hunt, isn't it?"

Shane's thoughts of Chelsea and Ella flashed back into his head. He nearly dropped the spoon; his mouth hanging wide open, his faced turned white.

"I'm sorry, son; I didn't mean to upset you."

Shane shook his head. "We were attacked—our camp was—they killed our guards and took our people, our families. I was the only one left, and I was trying to track them. I thought maybe if I could mark the trail and find out where they were going, well, then maybe—"

"You thought you could get 'em back?" Henry said.

Shane shrugged, grimacing from the pain in his shoulder. "We have more soldiers. I hoped I could lead them; show them the way."

Henry made a face and showed a nervous smile. "I'm sure you did the best you could, son. I saw the things you took down, and nobody could fault you for trying."

Shane changed the subject by pushing the bowl away from him. Again, he struggled to sit. "I have to get back out there; I can't let the trail go cold."

Henry nodded, showing his concern. "You need to rest, boy, get those fluids into you, then I'll go back out with you myself."

"No, I can't ask you to do that," Shane said, meeting the old man's tired gaze.

The old man smiled hesitantly as he stood and again checked Shane's IV bag, then retrieved the empty bowl from the nightstand. "I have to go. I know where they went…"

Chapter 8

On the road to Camp Cloud
Free Virginia Territories

The convoy bounced over the unmaintained logging trail as the stench of biodiesel exhaust leaked through rust holes in the deteriorating truck bed. Brad leaned over the side rail, gasping for fresh air. Between jolts, he looked out into the predawn forest to clear his head and let his thoughts catch up to the last twenty-four hours of activity. After months of downtime, he'd gotten lazy; not physically, but mentally. Days of routine tasks and the lack of adrenaline had changed him; now with things racing in all directions, he was struggling to focus, and he hoped the others wouldn't notice.

"We really should do something about this road," Brooks said with a grunt, his back bumping against the cab of the truck.

Brad turned, looking at his friend, crunched up and packed in with the others from the outpost. He nodded. "Priorities, I guess."

They were traveling as part of a four-vehicle convoy headed south toward Camp Cloud. Every able-bodied man from the Outpost, including Sean's original team, had volunteered to join them on the hunt. It wasn't entirely selfless; all the men having family and friends at Cloud made the mission an easy sell. Brad focused on the passing trees, wondering where the Primals were. Out in the open in a noisy truck, he expected to spot one or two. Usually, they would move out of the shadows toward the trails to see moving vehicles; it was one of the reasons they rarely used them for travel these days.

"Battle at Cloud stirred them up. Probably looking for these guys, same as us," Brooks said, reading his mind.

"All of them?" Brad asked.

Brooks grimaced with another bounce of the truck. "Most activity we've had around here in a while. Joe said the camp popped all of their flares. I imagine it brought everything in. Any of them living within eye shot of those flares would'a come running. I don't think they can help it… Damn things love flares." Brooks chuckled. "Don't worry; if I'm right, we're going to see more than our fill once we start tracking."

Brad shook his head and turned back. "How could so many from this faction have gotten this close to us without us noticing?"

"We've gotten soft, brother; stopped the daily patrols." Brooks paused to stuff a hunk of jerky into his cheek. "We started thinking we were secure out here."

"The men I put down at the safe house?" Brad said. "I don't think they were all together; they might not have even really known each other."

Brooks looked thoughtfully down at his boots, then turned back to Brad. "Sean figures the group that fired on him yesterday may have used some of the holdouts. You know… the prepper families still doing their own thing up on the mountain. He thinks they may be using those remote cabins to stage. They'd be well stocked and — "

A bright flash and thunderous boom from ahead shook through the convoy. The truck they were riding in slammed to a stop as debris and smoke rained over them. Gunfire erupted from farther up the trail, the loud call of an M60 machine gun. "Out! Out! Everyone out!" someone screamed. Brad hesitated, still stunned by the blast, then pulled his rifle to his chest. A man behind him leapt forward and caught rounds to his chest, screaming as he fell.

Brad took a deep breath and, finding the pause in firing, rose up, then dropped over the edge of the vehicle's bed, falling the way a scuba diver would leave a boat. He hit the ground hard and awkward just moments before another salvo of rounds sparked and pierced the sides of the truck's body. Brad forced his chest into the cold snow and mud, then leopard crawled forward until his face was against the embankment and the narrow rise in the earth provided cover. The sounds of the machine gun were now being joined by the return fire of men on the convoy.

By that time Brooks had managed to

circle around the truck, he was calling out directions with a knife hand, screaming for the men to rally and push into the ambush. "Move up! We gotta suppress or we'll lose everyone." Brad crept over the lip of the embankment and looked into the distant muzzle flashes, then fired an entire magazine in their direction before dropping back into cover.

A whistle and cracking of the overhead tree limbs was followed by an explosion behind him. "These fuckers have mortars?!" Brad yelled in disbelief. Finishing his reload, he climbed up to his knees. Brooks moved up alongside him, still calling out targets with his rifle as he fired into the direction of the enemy machine gun's fire. Brad looked down the column of shattered vehicles and could see that the men ahead were effectively pinned down, trapped in the kill box. More explosions thumped in from behind them and were getting closer as the enemy mortar men zeroed in on their location.

Brooks brazenly stood and fired. "Return fire. Push back!" he shouted to the men scrambling for cover in the muddy surface of the road all around him. He turned and grabbed

Brad by the collar, shaking him. "We have to flank that gun or they're all dead." Brad clenched his jaw and dipped his chin. The SEAL replied with the tightening of his brow and darted into the darkness of the trees with Brad following close behind.

They moved perpendicular to the road. Once far enough away that Brooks was sure they hadn't been spotted, he slowed his pace and then turned to again face the direction of the rattling machine gun. Brooks pointed into the darkness of the woods. They'd moved far enough into the trees so that they would now be on a rear approach to the machine guns, but the direction of travel would dangerously expose them to cross fire. Brad looked left and right; he could hear their own people in the convoy still firing, the mortar rounds exploding, the detonations getting closer together as the gunners homed in on their target.

The SEAL loaded a fresh magazine in his rifle then checked the slide on his pistol. "We don't have time to pussyfoot around; we've got to take the fight to them in a hurry. I bet there are only a pair of shooters, a spotter, and a couple of damn machine guns. We can do this, Army. You ready?"

"Waiting on you, squid," Brad spat back.

The SEAL smiled, showing his teeth through the matted hair of his beard. He pulled his rifle into the pocket of his shoulder and launched himself directly toward the sounds of the gunfire. Brad let him move ahead then, guiding right, took off on a path of his own. They were moving fast, yet staying low, knowing there was an enemy here that would not hesitate to kill. He allowed Brooks to move away, leaving only a few yards between the two men. They had to get on the attack; they'd allowed the ambushers to take the initiative and he could see by the intensity on Brooks' face that he wanted it back.

Rounds zipped and snapped through the trees overhead, the echo of the M60s scattering the report of the weapon across the leafless trees. Brooks was already firing before Brad saw the machine gun. He followed the direction of the man's rifle and watched the rounds impact with the berm of an improvised fighting position. As predicted, two men had dug into a V-shaped trench at the top of a crest overlooking the road. The mouth of the V faced the road and a machine gun on a tripod had been strategically placed at the end of each leg. Brad raised his rifle and began firing into the nearest machine gunner, his rounds hitting all around but none on the target. He prepared to bound to another tree when Brooks shouted for him to hold position.

The first machine gunner went down; the second was fighting with his weapon to try to turn it in Brad's direction. Before the man managed to make the adjustment, Brad's rounds finally found the gunner at the base of his neck. The man let out a gurgling scream as he fell back into the trench, pulling the weapon down with him. Foot falls in the forest alerted them to the spotter. They spun together and caught the flash of movement. The spotter was gone. Not another mortar round fell. But when Brad went to step after him, Brooks again called out.

"Don't move!"

"What the hell? You want to let him go?" he protested.

"It's not that; it's the claymores sitting right in front of us," Brooks said, pointing out a green object taped to the base of a nearby tree. "If these guys knew what they were doing, we would have already tripped it. Watch your feet, the wire's gotta be close."

Now fixated on the mine rigged for a tripwire at the base of the tree, Brad's eyes dropped to the ground. A clear filament line, just barely visible in the low light, was woven around the base of the surrounding trees. Brad followed the string and saw where it crisscrossed just two paces in front of him. He sighed and took a step back. "There," he said, pointing.

Brooks nodded and crept in, cutting the line with a pair of clippers stuck into the front of his vest. With the mine safe, he stepped forward and examined the setup before cutting the tape that secured it to the tree. "Good idea, poor execution. They put way too much confidence in this little booby trap."

Brad looked at the location of the mine and let his eye travel to the site of the hastily constructed machine gun nests. "They put it a little close to their hole, didn't they? That tree probably would have taken their heads off if it had exploded."

"These were for Primals sneaking up on them; they were too arrogant to suspect we'd flank. And I doubt whoever the spotter was cared if this crew walked away." The big man nodded and stepped closer to the trench. He dropped to the edge and looked down inside. "Come take a look." Brooks leaned over and picked up the nearest machine gun. "This is ancient and rusty as hell. And look at these two. Not the pros I was expecting; they're fat and wearing ragged camo."

"Well, they weren't dummies; they managed to mess us up," Brad said, waving a hand toward the battered convoy. He moved closer and looked down at the crumpled man in the trench. A strand of uncoiled wire attached to a small car battery was in the bottom of the hole.

"Someone set this up for them. I figure the one we wanted is back there," Brooks said, pointing in the direction the spotter fled.

Having heard the guns go silent, Brad

glanced up at the road and saw his men approaching the nest. Sean was leading the group with the Ranger behind him. Others were staying away, tending to the wounded and setting up security.

"What did you find?" Sean barked as soon as he was within range.

"Two shooters — look like mountain types. I figure whoever set this shit show up bailed out. Probably was parked someplacc in between here and the mortars," Brooks said, turning away. "They set up a claymore here to cover the back trail. If I had to guess, there's probably another mine over there."

"Could you find him?"

Brooks shook his head and pointed down at the series of scuff marks and boot prints headed up into the mountain. "The spotter? Piece of cake. What are you thinking?"

Sean turned back to the burning convoy. "I thinking I'm tired of walking into traps. I'm ready to go hunting."

Chapter 9

The old man stood in front of a wood-fired, kitchen stove, carving strips of meat from a carcass and dropping them onto a smoking skillet. Shane looked around the well-furnished farmhouse. On the first floor he could see that the windows were all covered by heavy planks. Lanterns burned, casting a soft, orange light and giving off the scent of kerosene. Looking around the kitchen, he could see mason jars filled with vegetables and a bin stacked with potatoes.

"I don't understand. So, you know all about the Camp, but you still stay out here all alone?" Shane asked.

"Sit," Henry grunted as he finished slicing the last bits of meat from the rabbit's frame. "What do I need the camp for? What would it do for me?" he said, turning away to wash his hands in a basin. Shane walked to a small kitchen table and eased into a high-backed chair. He watched as the old man turned to a tall pantry cabinet in the corner and unlocked it with a skeleton key from his pocket. Inside were Shane's weapons. "I didn't find but the one magazine for the rifle and it's near empty," he said, dropping the M4 and M9 on the table in front of Shane.

The weapons were spotless and oiled, all of the mud and grime removed. "You cleaned them?" Shane reached for the rifle and dropped the magazine, counting out five rounds before reloading. He locked the magazine back into the receiver. "Do you have any more ammo for it?"

The old man shook his head. "No use for it. I'll loan you my Winchester 30-30. I have a few boxes of cartridges to spare. I'll take your toy rifle as a deposit," he said with a smirk. "That's an old gun there—antique by most standards—but she shoots true and has more knock down than that little thing you was carrying."

Shane looked at the M4 and held it up. "It's not mine. I took it off a dead man."

"Hmm," Henry grunted. Nodding his head, he removed the meat from the skillet and placed it on a platter, along with thinly-sliced, fried potatoes. He dropped the platter to the center of the table and then took a seat opposite Shane. Henry looked down and closed his eyes, saying a silent prayer before snapping up to serve the meal. "So these people, the ones you called raiders, you never seen 'em before?"

Shane held his plate while Henry shoveled an even portion onto it. He looked toward a boarded window like he was solving complex arithmetic. "No, never."

"Really, how's that? They attacked without warning. They didn't ask for nothin'?"

"No, they attacked in the night; they didn't ask, but they sure took plenty," Shane said, his voice rising.

Henry chewed then gulped water from a glass. "There were a lot of them you said?"

"It was dark, but there were more than I could count. And they — they were trained; like an Army. They had mortars and machine guns. They moved so fast — even before we spotted them, they were at the walls." Shane dropped his fork and again turned to the boarded window. "I was with someone on the wall. We were talking when they attacked, we tried to fall back... back to get Ella. They were so fast."

"You said that name while you were out. *Ella*, is she your daughter?"

Shane bit his lip. "Something like that."

"Is she okay?" Henry asked, looking Shane in the eyes.

He shook his head. "I couldn't get to her—... honest, I tried. I made it to our building, but they were already inside... they were taking them."

"Taking?"

"There was nothing I could do. I wanted to fight them, but I didn't want to hit the girls, and there were so many... I watched them take the kids."

Henry held up a hand. "Just the kids? What about the rest?"

Shane dipped his head and closed his

eyes. "I don't know. I hid under a building and watched them. They grouped everyone together, then separated them. I saw one group move this way with the children, so I broke away and followed."

"And the rest, Shane? What did they do with them?"

Shane slowly shook his head side to side. "You said you knew where they were; when can we leave?"

Henry scooped the last of the food into his mouth. He chewed silently, watching Shane's face. He swallowed and took another drink from the glass, then exhaled. "Those men, the ones you're looking for, they're over the hill in a small village. The locals used to call the place *Crabtree*. Not many lived there before all of this, and the place went empty after it. There are train tracks that run through it; sometimes I would walk the tracks and collect lumps of coal for my stove."

Shane sat silently, allowing the man to continue.

"Never was much of a place, *Crabtree*. Corner store, a gas station, a couple, two, three houses. An old farm where an old man thought he'd try growing t'backer. The only thing the place ever had going for it was a railroad depot, but that sorta faded away with the coal mines.

"When the things happened and people started getting sick, the residents lit out of there—moved to high ground, I reckon; maybe to consolidate with friends or family farther up in the mountain. The Hill folks are like that, ya know.

"I visited a few months ago, t'was a ghost town. Doors locked, windows shuttered, every drop of fuel pulled from that gas station, shelves stripped from the store; the folks left nothing when they hightailed it. But that was then. It's not empty now. There's a lot of people there, and they've got a lot of stuff. Trucks, motorbikes, lots of guns. A raggedy fence surrounding the entire place. But mainly they got lots of people."

"You know them?" Shane asked.

"Oh, no. I've watched them from afar, but I don't know 'em. I suspect I know the type though," the old man said. Pushing back in his chair, he pulled a pipe and leather pouch from his pocket. "Like I said, I keep to myself up here on this mountain. But I recently had cause to give Crabtree another visit, to get closer. And what I found did concern me."

"Cause?"

Henry nodded as he stuffed tobacco into the pipe and packed it. He put the end into the corner of his mouth and looked back up at Shane. "The cause? Yup, three of 'em, and they're buried out behind my barn."

Shane's mouth fell open. "Buried?"

"Yup." He paused and lit a match. Puffing the pipe as he drew the flame over the tobacco, once it was smoking and glowing red, he took in a full lung and blew it out. "Vera never let me smoke in the house." He smiled and chuckled to himself. Placing the pipe back at the corner of his mouth, he continued. "They come by here a week or so ago, looking for the house. I had warning because they missed it the first two times. I was out in the back forty sitting in my tree, hunting boar. They done walked right below me. Walked right past, not knowing that I was up there. Something was off about the strangers, so I didn't bother calling out.

"I didn't know then that they was searching for my place in particular. They moved along and went back down the mountain, but they come back the next day. This time it looked like they were definitely after something; they had a map with my place on it. And when they found it, they done made camp about a quarter mile from here. I crept up in behind them and listened to 'em giggling. Planning and scheming, calling dibs on whatever family might be in the house. Who'd get pick of my guns and my food. One of 'em thought awful high of himself, he was the one giving the orders. The other two called him *Boss*, and he seemed to enjoy the title. He knew my name, knew my family.

"I held back and let them do their talking, have their fun. You know, give 'em a chance to change their minds and what not." Henry paused and leaned back. Reaching into the pantry cabinet, he removed a small bottle and two glasses. Shane waved him off. Henry nodded his understanding and returned one of the glasses. He pulled a cork and filled the glass with dark liquid. "You know, most folks don't bother aging their whiskey. But I did, and that's why I have barrels of it when most folks have jugs." He held up the glass and made a silent toast before sipping.

"These folks, they was up to no good. Two of 'em crept up to the house all quiet like, leaving the boss behind 'em. Then they started shouting, yelling for whoever was inside to come out. Come out, or they would burn the place, they said. All the while, I was sitting out there the shadows, sitting right behind 'em without them even knowing it."

"You killed them?"

Henry took another sip, let out a long breath, and shook his head. "Not all of 'em—not right off, anyhow. Now, you got to understand, boy, it give me no pleasure doing it, but some folks need to be kil't. Some folks are better off that way. Like a dog that gone bad, they can't be allowed to run free; you gotta put them down."

Shane exhaled shakily. "I understand."

The old man dipped his chin and took

another sip. "Once the first two got close to the house, I crept up behind the boss. Popped him at the back of the neck with my camp axe. He went down easy as a rotting tree. Then I just sat there and waited. The other boys, they kept calling back to the boss. The way stupid young'ins do, asking what to do next. Not able to act on their own. I just sat there and waited.

"It was dark by then, so I put on the boss man's hat and parka and stood by a tree. I let one of them fellers get in real close, then I stuck my knife up to the handle through his neck. It got real quiet then. That last boy, he seemed to wise up; he figured things weren't going his way and decided to cut out."

"I'm guessing he didn't get away."

Henry shook his head. "Stepped in a bear trap back behind the house."

"Jesus, Henry — a *bear trap*? What the hell?"

The old man shrugged. "You try living out here all alone for two years; a man's only got so many eyes. There's a path back behind the house; it runs up toward my still, then curves around toward the downside of the mountain. I reckon he was just following the trail to get away—doubtful that he knew anything about the still. The trap was just coincidence, but I won't complain, because it saved me from hunting after him all night."

Shane shook his head. "I guess it worked out for you, then," he said sarcastically.

Henry took another sip of the whiskey. "Yeah, I reckon it did," he answered simply.

The old man curled his fingers and pulled at his beard. "He stepped on it in the worst way, both legs, thing near cut 'em off at the knees. Not much I could do for him. I give him some whiskey and let him talk. Fella said his name was Ricky. Said he wasn't from these parts, that he come from Ohio. Just here doing what he had to, trying to stay alive, keep his family fed. He had a good story, I'll give 'em that."

"Ohio," Shane said.

"Yeah, and the other one from Wisconsin. The boss man, he said, was from Pennsylvania."

"What the hell are they doing down here?"

"Ol' Ricky claimed not to know the big picture; said that he was just following orders. He said they came into his camp a bit over a month ago. Said he was from a community outside Columbus. These people moved in during the night, killed most of the men, then offered the others a single opportunity to join up. Any that refused or hesitated were shot on sight."

"Sounds farfetched—did you believe him?"

"I've heard of armies in history doing worse. He claimed he had to join up or starve. Any man that joined, their family was left alone. Man claimed he had a wife and young boy back in Crabtree, and that if he messed up, they would pay the price for it. Said they was all headed to Texas and taking everything in-between. Said it was like Sherman's march to the sea. They take what they want and burn the rest, allowing some to join as they moved on." Henry paused and looked across the table. "What do you think of that? It sound like the ones that attacked your people?"

Shane nodded and looked down at his empty hands. "The boss, the one you said wore gray? I seen some others like him at the attack on our Camp. Who are they? What sets them apart from the others?"

Henry stared at the whiskey and swirled it in his glass. "Ricky said they were called Captains. Some with military experience, some police. Just ones they promoted up in their ranks to take charge of the new fellers until they were ready."

"Why would they come here? It's so far off the path, just like Camp Cloud. Why bother all of us?"

"They're taking every homestead, killing and leaving nothing behind. He told me about Crabtree, how they'd moved in. You know they picked it because of the railroad? They're riding trains down from Ohio. My guess is they plan to turn Crabtree into a station of sorts."

"We need to stop them. When can we leave?" Shane asked.

"Can you ride?"

Shane shot him a puzzled glance. "Ride?"

"A horse; can you ride?"

The young soldier looked across the table and nodded.

"Then we'll go in the morning."

Chapter 10

Free Virginia Territories

After more than two hours on the trail, Brooks turned toward a steep slope and took a knee. Sean was quickly at his side; he raised a gloved hand and signaled for the men to rest. Brad dropped in at the base of a tall oak tree where there the slope, sheltered by thick vegetation, had little snow. He turned so that his back was against the tree and removed his canteen.

Sean ordered the remaining vehicles and wounded back to Camp Cloud. They sent the Afghan scouts ahead on foot to root out any surprises and clear the route. Whoever attacked the Camp was going out of their way to delay their movement. It was a risk to split their force to go after the spotter, but it was also unexpected. Sean wanted to break their lines and put the raiders on the defensive.

The group was down to six plus the Texas

Ranger—a bit more than a reinforced fire team, but exactly what Sean wanted. All familiar faces to Brad. Brooks and Joey Villegas were up front on point talking with Sean. Looking out to the rear, he knew Cole—armed with a Squad Automatic Weapon—would be dug in and listening for anyone trying to sneak up on them. If anything got in behind them, he would lay down heavy fire, allowing the rest of the team to get online. Hassan backed Cole up; more tactful, the man could move like a ghost and make silent kills. Originally, Sean had wanted Hassan, the leader of the Afghan Scouts, to lead the wounded convoy back to Camp, but the skilled warrior refused. He insisted that at least one of their own be on the rescue party. Reluctantly, Sean agreed.

The chief looked back and silently ordered the patrol back to their feet. All of them up and moving without making a sound. The last eighteen months of living and hunting on the mountain had turned them into expert woodsmen. Woodsmen combined with the soldiering skills of a previous life made them a dangerous adversary for anyone that was willing to antagonize them. And that was exactly what these men had done. They'd stirred a hornet's nest of light fighters no longer constrained by the rules of war. They took their families and killed their friends. He didn't know how Chelsea was doing, and Ella and Shane were both missing. Brad squeezed the pistol grip of his rifle in an attempt to compartmentalize the anger brewing in his stomach.

They stopped again, this time taking a knee before crawling into the thick vegetation, while Joey scouted a game trail ahead. Earlier, Sean had briefed all of them, laid out a map, and tried to anticipate where the spotter and mortar team may have fled. A narrow cut wended from the main highway all the way through the valley. The road splintered and branched off all along the ridgeline and valley where homesteads and a small hunting cabin were scattered. Clouds' place was near the mouth of the valley where two roads forked; one side running east through his farm before turning north to the Camp and Outpost, the other guided west, eventually meeting a small river and passing several small mountain communities and again rejoining a main interstate. If they kept their current course up and over the slopes, they would intersect that trail before sundown — directly where the tracks were taking them.

Looking up, Brad saw Sean making a circling motion with his hands to call the men forward. *Joey must have found something*, he thought as he passed the word back. He watched Hassan and Cole materialize out of the brush behind him, and waited for the distance to close before standing and creeping forward. Joey was kneeling over a patch of snow, drawing a small diagram. Burt and Sean were beside him with Brooks, still glued to his rifle, looking out over the top of the slope and providing security.

Joey poked a finger in the snow four times and said, "I found the *cabrones*, held up less than a klick from here." The marine rifleman moved his hand away and dragged it over the snow, creating a long waving line. "The stupid bastards are camped right off the trail with no damn cover. They've got no idea we're following them."

"How many?" Sean asked.

"Four; one with a gray military parka, the

other three in rags. They're all gathered around a fire, warming their asses."

"Equipment?"

"Light rifles, heavy packs. Spotted a sixty mike tube." Joey paused to accept a water bottle from Cole. He took a long sip, then looked back. "Chief, these cats look rode hard and put away wet. You want, I'll go put them down myself."

Sean grinned and looked up at the sky then back down at his watch. "We got time for that. Break out the NODS; we're about to find out who the fuck these guys are."

The marine nodded his head. "We taking scalps or prisoners?"

"I want Gray Parka alive; we kill the rest," Sean whispered. "Joey, I need you to creep back up and keep an eye on them; someplace high to the right side of the trail. If they move, I want to know."

"Aye, Chief," Joey said.

"The rest of you, drink, eat, rest. As soon as the sun goes down, we move in."

Brad turned on his rear and eased back to his boots, moving back to his hide spot. He pulled his NODS and night scope from his kit and readied them for the attack. He pushed back into the base of the tree and stretched his legs. From his pack he removed a poncho liner, which he draped over his shoulders as he gnawed away on bits of beef jerky he kept in a folded scrap of waxed cloth. He forced his body to rest while his mind raced. Who were they? Most of what he'd seen had been amateurs, rookies, but some of them were different. Did they have professionals in their ranks? Would they be asleep, smoking, or not on watch at all?

With his back pressed to the tree, he watched the sun go down. His legs began cramping from the snow. He dropped the goggles over his eyes and watched the dark landscape transform into hues of green and black. He heard the crunch of snow and saw Cole and Hassan move to his location. Having stashed their packs back in the hide locations, the men were already geared up for the fight. Brad did the same with his gear and took the offered hand from Hassan.

Sean was kneeling at the crest of the hill with Brooks and the Ranger. Brooks smiled at Brad and pointed off into the thick forest. In the distance, they could see the glowing ball through the trees. Brooks leaned close and whispered, "Arrogant tools; that fire will broadcast their position for a mile or more."

Sean put a finger to his lips, then turned to them. "We'll line up on the ridge overlooking their camp. Villegas is already perched in close. I'll be down there on the ground so watch your targets. Sergeant Thompson you're with me."

Brad pitched back, surprised at hearing his rank and title. "What?"

"We need to take that leader alive, and I need Brooks on over watch with his rifle." Sean paused again to look them over. "Brooks will initiate. Remember, the leader stays alive!" The men nodded a reply and Sean stood with Brad falling in close behind. The team moved out along the top of the ridge, following a narrow path, Joey's footsteps in the snow barely visible. Sean led the way, walking straight up with his rifle in front of him but taking care to avoid branches and limbs. The moon was lost in the clouds; nobody would see him tonight, especially those gathered around a bright, burning fire.

Twenty meters from Joey's observation post, the men split off. Brad followed Sean while the others continued on to form a skirmish line along the ridge. Sean cut left and shuffle-stepped onto the downward slope, then stopped to survey the area. The fire was brighter here, nearly washing out Brad's night vision. He reached up and pulled them away from his eyes and was able to see down into the campsite less than half a football field away.

Previously, Brad had wondered if the men were professionals. Now, seeing the raider's camp at the base of a hill, surrendering the high ground, and burning a bright fire with no perimeter lookouts, he knew the answer. The men were reckless. The leader, identified by his gray parka and black watch cap, was sitting at the base of the fire with a bottle in his hand. Parka was talking in hushed tones to another across from him. The second man looked barely awake, wrapped in a striped wool blanket. Two more men were in sleeping bags on either side of the fire. Sean turned to Brad; with their faces only inches away, he said, "Boozing it up around a campfire. Let's slip around behind and wait for one of them to take a piss."

Brad nodded his response and dropped the goggles back over his eyes. The real threat here was noise. Brad searched the terrain carefully, placing every footfall like a surgeon. With the pre-action jitters filling his senses, every noise was now intensified. He could hear the creaking leather of his boots, Sean's breathing, the snapping of the campfire, and the muted laughing of the whispering men. Sean guided them just along the outside of the clearing the raiders had chosen to make camp in. Brad could tell they were more worried about Primals when they selected the place. More concerned with standoff than concealment.

They thought staying in the center of a natural clearing with a man on either side of the fire would allow them to see anything coming. Brad shook his head, just wishing a horde would break through and prove the arrogance of the men wrong. It seemed a waste to put them down so easily when a Primal horde would be far more poetic. Sean moved into a depression and Brad followed, crouching beside the chief. He continued looking at the group around the fire. What was once apathy, now slowly turned to anger.

This was the group that killed the men on the convoy. They were probably part of the same group that attacked Camp Cloud. They stayed behind to ambush anyone that came to provide support. Even with their advance weaponry, they were nothing more than street thugs, feeling confident with their strength in numbers. These were just punks; punks playing the bully while holding a rifle. Brad gritted his teeth at the thought of how these men were about to be taught a hard lesson in tactics.

It didn't take long before the man with the gray parka tossed the empty bottle into the fire and stood up. He stretched his arms and shifted his head from left to right. Brad watched as the man took a staggered, clumsy step back then walked to the nearest sleeping bag and gave it a kick. He stood over the man and barked, "Wake up! It's your watch."

The sleeping bag shuddered and turned

before it was yanked down from a pale face. The man looked up at the leader wearily, then dropped his head back down, moaning. The leader grunted a laugh, then slung his rifle over his shoulder, walking to the tree line. Sean silently passed his rifle back to Brad and dropped into a crouch. Through the thick beard and the shadows, Brad could barely make out Sean's features, though the man's dark hide jacket made him look like a mountain man from old movies. Sean turned and took two steps to the edge of the clearing and waited.

The leader in the gray parka seemed to walk directly toward them. The man fidgeted with his trousers. Staggering and nearly tripping, he turned and veered off to the right. He stepped to the tree line and extended an arm, bracing himself against a tree as he urinated into the brush. Sean crouched out of cover and took three big steps. The man gasped and flinched at the sound, air hardly escaping his lungs before Sean was on him. He wrapped a big gloved hand over the man's mouth and nose, blocking the oxygen. With a back trip and an under hook, Sean flipped the man through the air, crushing him face down into the fresh snow before planting a knee in the center of his back.

With hardly a *swish* and a *thump*, the raiders were left un-alarmed. The man squirmed until he felt the cold steel of Sean's blade pressed against his closed eye. "We going to have a problem?" Sean whispered. The man struggled to breath and Sean relaxed his grip on the man's mouth allowing him to speak. He yelped loudly, and the seated man at the camp fire looked up. There was a pop from the ridge above, just louder than the snapping of a branch. Before the seated man could recognize the danger, the top of his head was gone and his body had slumped forward into the fire.

The sleeping bags stirred and were quickly peppered with more suppressed gunfire from the ridge. Brad rose to his feet to find that the fight was over, three raiders dead, and the leader's hands zip tied behind his back, his ankles strapped together. "Well, Bozo, you just got your people greased. Nice work, asshole." Sean grabbed the man at the line between the man's feet and dragged him toward the fire pit. The man screamed out, causing Sean to turn back and plant a boot into the man's ribs. "You do that again and you'll eat my knife." The man looked back with wide eyes, the blood flushed from his face.

"Just let me go. I'll pretended nothing happened; nobody has to know," the man said.

Sean grinned. "Why would I care if anyone knows?" He shook his head side to side and laughed. He tightened his grip on the line and dragged the restrained man to the now motionless sleeping bag. He let the leader fall over the corpse of his man. Brad moved in and looked back, seeing the other members of the team moving out of the ridge line. The leader struggled and rolled to his back. Looking into the fire at the burning man, Sean used branch from the woodpile to work the body free, the dead man's burning coat sizzling against the snow.

The prisoner's eyes swiveled, finally absorbing the fact that his people were all dead. "Who are you?"

Sean grinned. Ignoring the question, he kicked the smoking body over and removed a small hand gun and knife from the man's belt.

"Jesus! Did you have to kill them?" the victim asked.

Sean stood and put his hands on his hips. Looking over the casualties, he shook his head, then tuned to face the bound man. "No. I don't even have to kill you, but I probably will."

The man leaned back, horrified, his mouth gaping as Brooks and the others gathered around the fire. Brooks didn't waste time; moving directly to the bodies, he made short work of stacking them together and dumping their pockets into one of the men's upturned caps. "Lots of good intel here, Chief. I doubt we need this sucker," Brooks said, moving to an empty stump. He sat down and began going through the cap. "Well now, what is this?" he said in an exaggerated tone, holding a folded sheet of paper. Villegas moved in and took the cap with the rest of the contents, opening a wallet, removing items, and one by one throwing them into the fire.

Brooks waved the paper in Sean's direction. "Yeah, this looks important, Chief."

"It's nothing," the man spat.

Brooks shrugged, holding the paper to the light and teasing that he might open it. Sean stepped closer and knelt down, giving a surprised expression. "It could be a map," he said. "Hell, just think; if this is a map back to your compound, then we don't need you."

"It ain't no map," the man rebutted.

Brooks held the folded paper up against the moon turning it slowly. "I don't know… looks like a map to me, Chief. Let's just shoot this guy and get moving."

"Fuck you. There ain't no damn map," the prisoner protested.

Sean grinned and moved closer, kicking a large chunk of firewood toward the bound man. He sat on the log facing him and rolled his shoulders before drawing an HK Mark 23 pistol from his holster. He pulled back the slide just enough to expose the glint of a .45 cartridge that he showed to the prisoner. "So, how confident are you that it isn't a map?" he asked. "And before you say anything, just know that the only reason you're still alive is so you can tell me where you're camp is at."

The man shook his head. "I'm done talking to you. Shoot me if you want; I ain't telling you anything." The man looked away, grunting and struggling to sit up. Sean grinned and let him lay in the dead man's bloody bedding. He reached into a pouch on his belt and removed a long tactical suppressor. "So, what? You're like ninety percent sure it's not a map, and no fear of being shot in the groin?" Sean said, making a show of attaching the suppressor to the handgun.

"Groin? What the hell is wrong with you?"

"Oh, I think you know," Sean said, his voice now lower and more deliberate. "You took some things that belonged to us. And we want them back."

Another grunt, "I can't help you with that. Besides, even if I told ya, you'll kill me anyway."

Sean turned and nodded to Hassan, who was eagerly standing just behind them with a length of rope. The Afghan scout swooped in and quickly tied the rope around the prisoner's neck, then lashed the other end around a heavy bit of firewood — heavy enough that the man could still carry it, but with difficulty. The man fought against his bindings, straining against the tension of the rope. "What the hell are you doing?"

"We're leaving you behind, but the level of cooperation you give will determine the condition we leave you in." Sean got to his feet and stepped closer before kneeling, then pressed the end of the suppressor into the man's crotch. His free hand grabbed the man's windpipe and squeezed. The prisoner flailed to escape his grip as his eyes filled with real fear and he fought for air. Sean relaxed his grip and allowed the prisoner to break free.

"No, no, please stop," the man gasped.

Sean eased back then scowled. "Tell me where the damn camp is or I'll blow your nuts off and leave you here for the Primals." Snarling his words, he pelted the man's face with spit as he dug in the barrel of the pistol.

The man pulled back, looking away. "I

can't tell you something I don't know."

Sean eased away the weapon, giving the prisoner instant relief. He turned to look at the team gathered around him. Away from the fire, keeping watch, Brooks turned to look back, holding up the scrap paper. "I say if this is a map, we shoot him in the face and get the hell out of here. Even in the cold, Chief, the Primals will be on us soon."

"Okay, okay, go east," the man gasped. "I'm telling you it's east, just let me be."

Villegas shook his head, tossing empty wallets to the fire. He moved closer, holding up a stack of driver's licenses. "Nah, this *hombre* is full of shit. I've been east; ain't shit that way but more mountain." He stepped closer and handed Chief a set of driver's licenses. "All three dead men are from Ohio. I bet this guy is too. Just shoot this fool, Chief."

Sean reached back and took the IDs, flipping through them. "Ohio, really?"

The man nodded his head violently, still gagging, his neck already beginning to bruise. "Yeah, so what? Most of the boys are from Ohio, but that don't mean nothing. I'm telling the truth—go east a ways; you'll find a trail. That's where they're at."

"How many?"

The man's eyes locked onto the pistol in Sean's hands. "You might just as well kill me, 'cause if I tell you any more, Carson will hunt me down himself."

From the shadows, Burt stepped forward, grinning, "So there it is; the confirmation."

The man's gaze shifted. "Why you got this Ranger with you? Carson's declared war on Texas. You know that makes you all part of it. You all are fucked now."

Burt ignored the prisoner and looked at Sean. "Ohio makes sense if they followed the railway. If he is here, we got a chance to stop him. Kill him."

Sean nodded in agreement and turned back to the prisoner. "How many? Last chance before you eat a bullet."

The man shook his head.

"How many?" Sean asked.

The prisoner's eyes went wide before answering the question. "More than you can count."

Sean smiled. "And Carson?"

The man dipped his chin. "He'll kill you," he muttered.

Sean looked at Brooks. "What's on the paper?"

Brooks unfolded the scrap and looked at the handwritten note. He laughed and tossed the paper into the fire. "Some bullshit poem."

"Okay then, we go east," Sean raised the pistol.

The man screamed, "You said you'd let me go!"

Sean aimed low, firing a single shot that grazed the inside of the man's thigh just above the knee. A shallow wound that bled heavily. Sean tuned as the man wailed; with his bound hands, he rolled in agony. Chief put his arm in the air, making a lasso motion and gathering the men around him, then looked back toward the high ridge to the east and started moving, the others falling in behind him.

"What the hell we doing, Chief?" Villegas asked. "I told you there ain't shit this way."

Sean snorted. He looked back behind him to see the prisoner still rolling on the ground. "I know that. And he knows that. Once that man back there gets over his tantrum and figures we're long gone, he'll cut himself free with that pocket knife that I ignored in his back pocket."

Villegas grinned. "So, we ain't going east?"

Sean shook his head. "We're going just over the hill, Joey; then we'll follow that bastard home."

Chapter 11

"How's the shoulder?" Henry asked.

The old man was standing over a wash basin, wiping his hands with a cotton cloth. They'd just finished breakfast and the man had placed the now clean dishes on a rack over the sink. Shane was shirtless, sitting on a wooden chair near an open fireplace. His wound was closed, dull red scabs crusted over the black stitching. Jagged teeth had punctured deep into his skin, leaving a dark bruise below the collar bone. He was applying salve from a shallow tin, rubbing it over the scabs.

"It's a scratch," he said quietly. "Where did you learn to stitch?" Shane asked, running his fingertips over the hard, black sutures.

"Taxidermy," Henry answered, crossing

the room to take the salve from Shane. He placed a folded shirt over the back of the chair. "Fixed the hole in yer shirt. The critter that got ya had a hell of a jaw."

"Thank you," Shane said, rolling his shoulder.

Henry stepped away and looked down at him. "Sure you're up to traveling? I could go it alone."

Shane shook his head, slipping the shirt over his arms and shoulders. "I'm fine," he said, standing. The chair scooted back away from him. Henry had bags packed by the door, the lever action Winchester resting against the wall. Shane moved toward the gear and gripped the rifle, checking the action. On the stock was a leather sleeve with an additional twelve rounds.

Henry pointed to a heavy jacket with a sheep's wool collar hanging on a hook. "You'll need that too."

Shane reached for the range coat then paused. "Henry, why are you helping me?"

The old man smiled and stepped slowly

toward the stone fireplace. "Maybe you were right, maybe I am tired of being alone," he said, taking a .44 Henry rifle from a rack above the mantle. He moved across the room and took a seat on a walnut hall tree, then laid a leather holster across his lap and seated a 1911 pistol. "I guess after Vera died, I stopped caring about other people. I've been pretty content with just holding out up here and taking care of myself."

"And Vera, she was your wife?" Shane asked innocently.

Henry nodded and reached for a set of heavy leather boots.

"How did it happen? Was it the Primals?"

The old man glanced up from the laces he was tying. "The sick folks... 'Primals,' that what you call 'em?" he answered, shifting his feet. "Nah, but not for lack of trying. I tell ya, that woman could fight. I got some scars to prove it." He looked off and grinned again. "She was old, son, and wasn't even in the best of health before all of this started. The cancer most likely took her, but I don't know; once we lost contact with my son, I think she kind of lost her fight. She got tired." Henry flipped the gun belt over and filled leather stitched loops with ammunition from a box, then stuck the remainder into his pack.

"You have a son, then?" Shane asked in a low voice.

The old man looked off as he seemed to search for the answer. "Yeah," he said finally. Henry reached into his shirt pocket and began to pack his pipe. "He's in Charleston. Smart kid; he would have gone north with the convoys. We talked about it before the phones failed. I told him he should go. I told him to follow the soldiers north." He rolled the pipe in his hand and tamped it.

Shane looked down at his feet, reflecting on his own time during and after the fall — the chaos in the streets, the mad panic, and the lack of any organization from the government. He looked at the tired eyes of the old man. How would Henry have known what it was like out there? He'd been here on this mountain through it all. Shane knew the old man blocked out what must have happened to his son. Shane knew because he'd tried to do the same.

Henry struck a match and lit the pipe. He stood, then hoisted a pack with a bedroll strapped to the top. He pointed out an identical pack leaning against the wall, then took the pipe from his mouth and rubbed his leathered and worn hands together. "You mentioned the girl, that she is like a daughter, but do you have a woman?"

"No," Shane said stubbornly. "I have a friend. We got split up during the fight; she'll be back there waiting for me. But no, I don't have anyone… not really. She's just a friend."

Henry eyed him suspiciously and ran a hand through his gray hair. "Friend? What the hell does that mean? Damn, son, you either got a woman or ya don't."

"Then I guess I don't," Shane spat back. "Sometimes I wish I did, though."

The old man gnawed at the end of the pipe, giving Shane a skeptical glance. He shook his head and pointed to the pack and rifle. "Well, that's your gear. C'mon, follow me. I hope you weren't lying about being able to ride."

Henry hurried to the door and Shane followed him. The sun was a just over the horizon, but it wasn't bright; dark shadows still hung through the tall trees. Having been the first time he'd stepped outside Henry's home, Shane stopped and looked around. The place was well taken care of; snow covered flower beds and an old pickup truck topped with a canvas cover showed him Henry had maintained some semblance of his previous life. Off to the back, from what Shane could tell, was a staked off garden. Henry moved on, shuffling over a shoveled path toward a tall barn. As they approached, the horses detected them and began shuffling; Shane could hear them moving inside as the old man slid open a door.

Henry wasted no time grabbing gear from a post; he lifted a saddle, blanket, and bridle, then moved to a stall in the barn housing a pair of line back duns. The old man moved to the nearest and signaled for Shane to take the other. "Sally here, she's gentle enough for you; she was Vera's girl," he said softly. "She'll take care of you."

Shane reached for a second saddle and

bridle, and stood watching as the old man entered the stall. The man rubbed the horse's back and whispered to it before covering it with the blanket. The horse turned and moved closer, ready to accept the saddle. Henry worked efficiently and finished his task, then turned back to see Shane standing awkwardly with the saddle still in his hands. "Come on now, son, you got to work with me," he chuckled, taking the saddle from Shane. "I'll help you out this time, but a man needs to be able to care for his own horse."

Henry prepped Sally in no time, explaining what he was doing as he quickly prepared the horse for the day's ride. When the mare was ready, he took Shane's rifle and slid it into a long, leather sheath on the horse's right side. He walked the horse around and placed a rein in Shane's palm. "We'll walk them for a bit as they get used to the terrain, then we'll be on our way."

Shane waited a minute before asking, "You sure this is okay with the Primals? Won't they attack the horses?"

Henry nodded and rubbed his hand over

scars on the flank of his horse. Shane could easily recognize it as a human bite. "If we run into Primals, you just hang on; the girls don't like them anymore than we do. They'll get us out of trouble." Henry grinned. "But if you fall off and they get surrounded, you best clear out cause these girls will fight."

Shane nodded and stared at the horse as he put a hand to the scars. Henry moved out, leading the way down a snow-covered trail. When they'd cleared the farm's property, he stopped and swung into the saddle. Shane placed a boot in the stirrup and pulled himself up into place. Henry watched and smiled his approval. "Keep your sidearm where you can reach it; you don't have to do much else. Sally there will follow along, you just enjoy the ride."

They wended along a tract of flat land high with brown grasses, the edge lined with tall cedar trees. Henry waved a hand as he described his property lines and small improvements he'd made to the place since he'd lived there. Shane gripped the saddle horn and tried to adjust his body to the horse's stride. The trail narrowed and the trees closed in around them. The terrain grew difficult and Henry stopped speaking as he concentrated on navigating the path. The horses stepped heavily, seeming to carefully place each footfall to avoid slipping on the frozen ground.

Off to the left, the terrain dropped down away from them. Shane looked ahead and could see they were moving deeper into the valley; a notch at the end showed an opening far in the distance. White and gray clouds hung overhead, and a cold, damp air crept into the collar of his jacket. Henry moved them down the trail, which eventually dumped them onto a narrow road covered in untouched snow. At the far side of the road was another stretch of grass that butted up against a slow moving stream.

"There's good fishing here," Henry said casually.

Shane let his head drift left and right. It was empty, no signs of inhabitants or travelers, no homes, and no people. Just an enormous slice of land, untouched except for the road. The air was fresh, the sounds of the flowing water calming. He stiffened his shoulders, having to remind himself that the looks of the place could be deceiving, that danger always lurked close by. He grew up on a farm, hiking trails and traveling through the forest with his grandfather. He was no stranger to the woods and felt more at home here than in any city.

The horse swayed below him as it navigated a hole in the road. Far ahead, blue sky was beginning to reveal itself, and below that, in the opening of the trees, he could see the makings of a blacktop road where the sunlight had melted away the snow. Henry moved his horse to the center of the road and slowed so that they were now side by side. He reached into his pocket for his pipe and placed it into the corner of his mouth.

"I been pondering on this for a bit. I don't think we can expect much by sneaking up on 'em. Worst case, we get caught and shot for our troubles," he said, speaking softly.

Shane nodded, keeping his hands on the saddle horn. "Then what are you planning to do?"

Henry smiled. "I think we ride right up to the gate and asked to be let in. If they are in fact creating a settlement, they'll be looking for strong men." The old man turned and looked Shane up and down with a grin. "I'm sure they'll take me, and I can always put in a good word for you."

"What about the men you killed?" Shane asked. "I don't think these folks are friendly."

"Aye, but they are still folks; and folks is known to be curious," Henry said, chewing the end of the pipe. "Crabtree is just around the bend. Last I visited, they were building a fence and a gate at the base of the road."

"I don't know, Henry. I think I'd rather take these men on behind this rifle, but I'll give your way benefit of the doubt."

The old man nodded and lifted a hand, guiding his horse west onto the blacktop road. As they moved into the sunlight and over a narrow bridge, Shane could see the outline of Crabtree in the distance. The raiders had done more than build a fence; the small settlement was completely enclosed by a wall, complete with watch towers. Henry pointed to a bank of snow to the right of the road. "There's railroad tracks under that drift," he said. "I come this way to gather coal in the fall."

Shane nodded, not taking his eyes off the far away wall. He could see men moving in the towers as they took notice of the distant riders.

"There were good people that lived here; good people could live here again one day."

Shane shrugged. "You'd know more about that than me."

Henry laughed. "That's right, I forgot you ain't got a woman of your own. It tends to give a man a different perspective on things."

Shane saw heads appear over the top of the wall, followed by rifles leveled over the edge and pointed in their direction. Henry rode on, seemingly unconcerned with the attention. The sun was high and in line with the road, hanging just behind them. Shane laughed thinking of the sight of two men on horseback riding out of the sun toward a frontier outpost. He hoped the Raiders would find as much humor in it.

"What are you planning to tell them?" Shane asked.

"I'm sure I got a story or two left in me;

you just stay with me, son."

To Shane's surprise, he watched as the gate began to open and two men carrying rifles close to their chests stepped out. Henry picked up the pace and Shane followed, making tiny preparations in his head for the suicidal gunfight that he was sure was in store for them. He had no illusions that the people in Crabtree were killers and they would have little respect for a person like Henry, as peaceful as he may appear to be. Shane paused and tried to hold back his own grin… maybe Henry was the one these men should be afraid of.

A big man stepped from the cover of the gate and held up a hand to them. Broad-shouldered with wide forearms and easily over two hundred pounds. He wore a well-trimmed, red beard and a dark watch cap covered his head. The stub of a cigar hung from the corner of his mouth. He reached out with his hand, took the cigar, and spit onto the road. Shane studied the men's faces, none of them showed concern as they held their weapons down.

"That'll be close enough," Cigar said.

Henry pulled back on the reins, stopping his horse, and Shane's stopped with it.

The man stepped closer, eyeing the sheathed rifles strapped to the horses. "What business you fellas got in Crabtree today?"

Henry took the pipe from his mouth and flicked it against his wrist, knocking spent tobacco out. "I ain't here to see you, I'm here for the boss."

Cigar grinned but seemed to appreciate Henry's candor. "If you're here about a bounty, I'm the man you need to speak to."

"It ain't about the bounty — it's about the price."

The big man leaned back, letting out a loud laugh. "Ain't it always." He turned and slapped one of the guards on the back. Then waved a hand. "Open the gates. Show these two tough guys where they can put their horses, then bring 'em to me."

Chapter 12

Free Virginia Territories

When her patient began to stir, the brown-eyed nurse sitting at the end of the bed looked up from a basket of linen she was folding. Chelsea forced her eyes open, the blinding light sending shockwaves through her brain. The nurse rose and walked to the hallway, then returned with a tall man in a stained, yellow lab coat. The man moved close to the bed and looked Chelsea over. She was heavily drugged and could only faintly register his touch.

The man drew the sheet down from her chest and ran his hands along her rib cage then forced her jaw open and shone a light into her mouth. "She'll be okay. No more drugs, and when she wakes, make sure she eats something," the doctor said, turning to leave the room.

The nurse nodded as she wrote notes on a clipboard. Once the doctor left the room, she placed the clipboard on a table near the door, then pulled a chair closer to the bed. Knowing that Chelsea was awake, she asked, "Can you hear me?"

The nurse waited for a reply before she continued. "It's okay, you're safe now."

Chelsea crunched her eye lids together and nodded. She spoke in a dry, raspy voice. "Where am I? Is this a hospital?"

"No, this isn't a hospital. It's just a clinic. You're lucky the men brought you back or you'd be dead. You'll be okay now; the doctor saved you."

"Saved me?"

"Of course. They found you out there and brought you back. And soon you'll be on a train to New Philadelphia with the others. You've been rescued."

Feeling the heavy bandages tightly compressed around her body, she tried to raise a hand to her ribs. The nurse took her wrist and gently guided it back to her side. "You need to rest. The doctor said you were close to death when they found you; nearly frozen in that enemy camp."

Chelsea's eyes went wide with recognition as she remembered the battle. "Wait… the camp. Is every one okay?"

The nurse smiled and put a hand on Chelsea's arm. "They were able to rescue many of your people."

"When can I go back?"

"Why would you want to return? I told you; you're safe. Soon you will be sent to the city in the north. All of you will."

"I don't understand. Who are you? What is this?" she said, her voice growing raspy as the drugs faded and she could feel the squeezing tightness in her chest. The nurse stood and moved away. Retrieving a glass from an end table, she dropped in a straw and urged Chelsea to drink.

"My name is Angie. You're safe, now.

General Carson will make sure all of your people are taken care of. Just rest and you'll be reunited with them soon."

There was a knock at the door and a young man entered, holding a small tray of food. The nurse waved a hand toward a small table where the man left the tray. She stood and adjusted Chelsea's sheet so that it was tucked under her arms, then walked to the door. "I have other patients I need to tend to. After you eat, we can talk again."

"Wait," Chelsea said, raising a hand.

The nurse turned back and smiled. "Yes?"

Chelsea struggled to sit up. "Do you know who attacked us?" she asked.

"You poor thing. The doctor said you may have trouble remembering. You were not attacked, dear… you were freed from that awful camp."

Chapter 13

Free Virginia Territories

Cole and Brad sat together in the observation post overlooking the campsite. The temperatures had again dropped. Snow was falling steadily and over two inches had accumulated in the last three hours. The fire was smoldering, and the wounded man they were watching had managed to free his hands. He was now wrapping his gunshot wounds with cut strips from the dead men's bedding.

"No Primals yet," Cole whispered.

Brad nodded. "I was expecting them, too. They're out there, though; I can feel it."

Brad had known Cole the longest of any of them; a designated machine gunner on his vehicle in Afghanistan. A place that seemed to be on another planet now, in a different reality. The two of them had come so far and taken different directions getting to this snow-covered hole on a ridge in the Appalachian Mountains. He knew Cole had a family now; he'd seen him with a local girl a time or two and knew they were starting something together. Looking at his friend, he could see an unfamiliar worry in his eyes.

"She'll be okay," Brad whispered. "We'll get them all back."

The man pulled the SAW into his armpit and looked across at Brad. "I don't even know that she's there, Sergeant. She's a good girl, and I think she would have gotten away. Maybe made it down to Dan Cloud's cabin. We had a plan for escape, just like we were told to."

Brad forced a smile. "I bet you're right. She's a tough one. Is that old man of hers still giving you a hard time?"

"Hard as woodpecker's lips. He's just looking out for his daughter; I can respect that." Cole raised a hand to his lips then pointed at the campsite. "He's moving."

Leaning forward, they could see the wounded man had removed the binding and bandaged his leg. The snow around the campsite was painted in bright red blood everywhere the man had stepped. He was picking over the dead men's packs and stuffing items into a small knapsack. Brad watched as the man knelt by the fire and attempted to warm his hands over the dying coals. He turned his head and seemed to look directly at them. The man laughed and got to his feet, then turned to move west, leaving the clearing and entering the forest.

"Chief was right; the bastard was lying," Cole whispered.

Brad turned back and waved a hand to the others positioned in the low ground behind them. Brooks was up moving to the front immediately. Without speaking, Brad pointed out the direction of travel and Brooks swept down the hill without making a sound. Brad stayed in position, allowing Sean and the Ranger to pass before he got to his feet and dropped into the column. He heard the slight swish of movement behind him that he knew was Hassan and Cole finding their security positions in the back. Joey pressed up behind him and they moved out together.

Brad watched as the men ahead of him moved stealthily through the bush. Even the Ranger had skills of movement that Brad hadn't expected; it was hard to tell if they were the skills of a hunter, or just the things one picks up having survived two years in the apocalypse. They skirted the clearing of the campsite, sticking to cover, and easily found the man's trail. Even though the wounded man had attempted to bandage his wound, he was still dropping blood. Brooks had to stop them often, holding them back as they waited for the wounded man to rest.

Through the thicker woods of the forest, they merged onto a narrow trail that was marred with tire tracks of — most likely — smaller ATVs. They stayed moving west and down the mountain. At the bottom of a rise, Brooks halted them again and called Brad forward where Sean and the Ranger were kneeling beside the thick trunk of an elm tree. He moved in close and touched his glove to the thick triangle carved in the bark.

"It's one of ours," Sean said. "A day or two old at the most."

"Who left it?" Brad asked.

Sean removed his glove and scratched at his beard. "It'd be one of the troopers; they're the only ones that use the broad head sign. One of Turner's crew; only a handful of them were left back at the camp. Someone followed the raiders through here."

"Bread crumbs," Joey said, nodding.

"Could be Chelsea… or Shane," Brad said.

"Could be," Brooks said, spinning the cap from a plastic canteen. He took a drink and passed it to the man next to him. "Thing is, it looks like our trails are lining up. We're on the right path." He took the canteen back from Sean and replaced the cap. "But your boy is gassing out." Brooks pointed to the blood trail. "I'm surprised he's gone this far spilling all that Kool-Aid in the snow."

"How far away is he?" Sean said.

"Less than five hundred."

Brad took a deep breath, and fought back the anxiousness he was beginning to feel in his legs. Knowing they were getting closer and that his people were in trouble made him want to run. To do whatever it took to get them back. He sighed and forced his body to relax, shrugging to adjust the weight of his pack and rifle.

Sean stroked his beard and dipped his chin. "Stay with him as long as we can. If he falls out, we'll follow the marked trail."

Brooks stepped off, moving very slowly and deliberately now, pointing to the broad head symbols. The markings ran along through a depression with high ground on one side. He checked every footfall, moving in and out of the trees, avoiding the leaves. The wounded man struggled ahead; he'd all but stopped his movement. The team bunched up on the trail, following just behind the now belly-crawling man leaving a trail of blood. Given the man's condition, Brooks could have easily gotten closer unseen, but he chose to stay back.

The point man paused and put his eyes to

the sky, focusing on a distant sound. To the west, there was an unmistakable howl. The team froze at the same time as the crawling man. Brooks eyes searched the terrain. He removed his glove and put a hand to the air. After a moment, he turned back to face the team and pointed up the hill. "They smell the blood; the wind is taking it right to them."

Sean nodded in agreement. "We can hold the high ground."

The Ranger stepped out of the column and pointed to the wounded man ahead of them. "What about him?"

Sean shook his head. "None of our concern—"

Before Burt could protest, the lone howl turned into a chorus that was growing closer. "Those things are on the run. Get me a defensive perimeter on that hilltop."

Cole and Hassan were the first to bound forward, rushing for the high ground. By the time Brad closed in behind them, he could hear the brush to their back snapping as the Primals plowed through it. The low howl turned to screams as the creatures sensed prey. The man on the trail began to yell and plead for help. Sean ignored him, quickly setting up a defense, directing the men into a circle with the majority of the force looking downhill. Brooks lagged back, emplacing the salvaged claymore mines.

After setting the booby-traps, the point man took the hillside with bounding steps and dropped to his knees beside the others. Suddenly, it was very quiet. The howling stopped; the man below quit yelling. Brad had seen this before. The Primals had gotten smarter in the past year. They didn't always run head first into a storm of bullets the way they had during the fall—not at first anyway. He pulled the rifle to his shoulder and held his breath, searching the trees at the downside of the trial. As he focused, he could hear them moving around in the vegetation. The wounded man heard them too; he grabbed the last of his strength and tried to stand, limping toward the hilltop, before again falling and clawing at the dirt.

A big male stepped from the brush; he was completely nude, his chest and back covered in raised scars, and a heavy head of hair fell below his shoulders.

"They're here," Burt whispered.

"More where that came from," Sean answered. "They'll be right in those trees, waiting."

The Alpha Primal moved toward the downed man and stood over him with its head raised, sniffing and licking the air. It looked down at the man, then up the hill toward the dug in soldiers. Its head twitched back toward the trees before it arched its back and howled. More creatures ran from the dark forest and swarmed over the wounded man, his screams hardly breaking through the roar of the mob.

The man's cries of agony ended with a death rattle. A group of female Primals gathered the body and carried it back into the trees. The big male held its position, its eyes focused on the hilltop. Tucked into the shadow of a fallen poplar tree, Brad froze, trying to stay invisible. The big male took a heavy step to the hilltop; its head again raised sniffing at the air. Other males gathered around it and searched the face of the hill, spotting the broken earth and disturbed snow where the team had scrambled up. The nude male took another step and looked up, staring directly at the team as though trying to make sense of the shapes. Brad knew it was an Alpha Primal — it was the leader of this group — but it had made a fatal flaw, and its reign would end today if it moved any closer.

The creature raised its foot for another step. A click of a rifle's safety made the creature twitch; its foot fell and the forest floor exploded with the crash of the claymores. With a blast of thunder and flash of heat and light, a swath of forest to the front of the paired mines was vaporized by the 1,400 tiny ball bearings propelled forward. Earth and ice rained down all around them. Brad rose up, looking into the smoke below. Some of the creatures still moved, but most were destroyed and mangled by the blast.

"Move!" Sean ordered, snapping them all to their feet.

"Are there more?" Burt asked.

"I'm not waiting around to find out."

Brooks rose up and looked over his weapon, pointing into the trees. "There's more, boss, a lot more."

Brad stood, straining to see into the darkened forest. Creatures slowly materialized through the smoke, sheltered below in the trees. "Oh shit, we haven't seen these numbers in months," he gasped. As his eyes focused, five became ten, and ten became twenty; soon, he could see that the mass stretched far back into the forest. They'd stumbled on the edge of a massive herd.

"The fighting. All the activity is bringing them up the valley," Hassan said coolly from behind him. The scout stepped closer and drew a machete from his belt and stuck it into the ground, readying it for the attack. "They will come now."

A single howl quickly turned into a thunderous roar as the forest came alive with screams.

"We should run!" Burt yelled.

"Not today we won't. Too many to outrun." Sean shook his head, unsnapping magazine carriers on his vest. He shifted to the side, directing Cole to move his machine gun up. "We hold the high ground. We can do this."

"Are you serious?" Burt said incredulously, stepping behind the line.

Brooks looked back at him with a grin. "I hope you got your vaccination, cause shit is about to get bitey."

Brad felt his arms shake from the adrenalin; the creatures were drawing forward for an attack. "Why are they coming? They know we'll kill them." He swallowed as he pulled the tomahawk from his pack and stuck it into a nearby tree.

Joey laughed, prepping his own tomahawk. "Cause we killed the Alpha; now they're too stupid to know any better."

"When the first of them gets to the trail, open fire," Sean called from his flank position.

A bark from Brooks' rifle initiated the charge. All along the slope, the Primals emerged from the tree line, screaming and scrambling forward. Brad leveled his weapon and fired; before his victim could hit the ground, two more had pushed by it. He continued sweeping the front and firing rapidly, the collapsing bodies rolling down the hill and tripping up the others.

Soon the hillside was reduced to blood and mud. The creatures were on all flours clawing at the sludge, fighting to make their way up the slope. Joey stood and crept closer, firing his rifle into the tops of the heads. The Primals mixed in a tangled mess with the dead. Occasionally, a creature would find a foothold and bound forward, only to be rewarded with a gunshot to the face or a hack from Hassan's machete.

"Cease fire; save your ammo," Sean ordered when it was apparent the forward momentum of the mob had been lost. The remaining creatures were attacking the slope like a greased pole, some only making it halfway before losing traction and sliding back down. The herd had been reduced to under a hundred. Others on the tree line below were already pulling back, some dragging bodies of the dead with them.

Brad turned his head away as the copper scent of the blood mixed with the waste of the Primals made him wretch. The creatures' howls from below sent an involuntary shiver up his spine; he stepped back, retrieving his tomahawk from the log as he moved.

"You okay, boss?" Joey asked him.

Removing a canteen from his belt, he drank thirstily and said, "I'm fine. We need to move before they find another way up this ridge."

Sean agreed and signaled the group to remount their gear and move out, withdrawing in the direction of the broad head markers.

They traveled swiftly and it didn't take long before they came upon another sign of violence. At the bottom of a gulch, Brooks called them forward where he pointed out evidence of a Primal attack on a large deer. His hand swept over the torn up ground that signaled the high numbers of the crazies involved. Tufts of hair and fur were scattered around a bloody patch of snow.

"And there's more," he said, walking toward the high ground.

As Brooks moved passed a Primal body, he pointed to a spent brass cartridge under the thick brush sheltered from the snowfall. "Someone fought here." He continued on the trail, pointing out more of the dead before stopping at the remains of a man, a blood-stained body with a cut across its back and a fighting knife buried deep into the torso.

Sean stood over it and looked left and right. "Anything else?"

"A couple things," Brooks said in a hushed tone. "The broad heads stop here. This is where our guide made his stand."

Hassan moved to the bloodied body and rolled it over. He reached down and pulled the knife out to examine it. "This is no hunter's knife."

Sean pursed his lips and spit in agreement. "Then who left the marks? Where is he?"

Brooks paced farther up and rubbed the

back of his head, kneeling down he used his glove to sweep fresh snow from the trail. "Whoever it was, he was carried out of here… and on horseback. He went that way," He pointed away from the direction they were traveling in. "One rider with two horses. From the depth of these boot prints, I'd say our friend was carried out."

"Dead?" Sean asked.

Brooks shrugged. "No way of telling, but why haul off a dead man?" Brooks knelt and let his gloved finger rub the edge of the hoof print. "Why take a wounded man, for that matter?"

A distant howl turned their heads to the back trail. "No time to worry about it," Sean said. "Keep moving the way the broad heads indicated. Our mission stays the same; I want to find the bastards that attacked us."

Chapter 14

Crabtree wasn't much of a town, or a settlement. It lay stretched out between a small creek and a railroad bed. Two main roads ran through it and intersected near a long, flat building with a square overhang that could easily be recognized as a gas station. With the community now fortified and the roads blocked off, it wasn't much more than a cluster of buildings surrounded by an earth and timber wall.

The raiders had used a pair of bulldozers to build a high earthen barrier, then lined the outsides with vertical logs. In some places, the dirt was packed right against the community's buildings as high as the roof lines. Two tall sheet metal gates were placed where the railroad tracks ran through the fence. Another tall gate was placed where they'd entered earlier on the east side near the town's only road entrance.

The work had left the small community looking like a mess of trenches and mud. The stream that was sparkling clear on the ride in was now clouded with mud and soil. But, looking around, Shane had to agree the defenses looked efficient, and the high berms provided easy access to the tops of the inside wall. These people knew what they were doing and, by the looks of them, had done it before.

A short, skinny man, introduced as Bones, led them toward a big, red barn. Over the open doors was a faded sign that read *'Welcome to Crabtree'*, and people moved around outside the structure. Beyond it was the makings of a tent city and a sort of motor pool filled with an assortment of vehicles. A board walk made of logs wound between the tents and skirted a muddy dirt road. Smoke hung in the air from campfires. Henry leaned toward Shane and spoke softly. "They've been busy; this looks nothing like it used to."

Bones continued guiding them to the barn

and spoke over his shoulder. "You been to Crabtree before?" the man said, overhearing the comment.

Henry's eyes widened in surprise at having been heard. "Years ago. Passed through here as a young man."

"Ah, I see," Bones replied. He walked them to a split rail fence, then stopped to light a hand-rolled cigarette. "You can tie your ponies here," he said as he turned to face them, showing scabbed lips and buck teeth. He stood with his hands on his hips. "Like you said, we been busy, that's for sure. Can't loiter out in the frontier. We got the fence up as soon as we could, train will be here soon, and ya'll know Carson won't visit a post without a fence."

"Yup, you got that right," Henry bluffed. He sighed and approached the rail, using a mangers tie to secure the reigns. Without speaking, he slipped back around and retrieved a pair of feed bags. He gave one to Shane, then readied the horses. "What's with the barn? I don't like leaving my stock outside in the weather," he said, slipping the bag over his horse then retrieving his rifle from the leather sheath.

Bones turned and looked into the stable. "Barn's occupied at the moment, but I'm sure we could find you somethin' if you're fixin' on stayin'. Most of these outer buildings is empty for the time bein'."

Shane moved around Sally and stared into the open doors. "So, what's in the barn then?"

Bones turned back and looked him in the eye. "Nothin' for you to worry about. C'mon, Gus is waitin' on ya."

With the horses tied, Henry nodded to Shane and turned to follow the skinny man across the compound. To the west of the flat-roofed gas station was a country market, two stories and built mostly of red brick. Opposite that was an old, wood-sided farmhouse and, running along the road, two smaller homes with detached garages and outbuildings. Farther west on the main road was another pair of warehouse-shaped buildings that sat alone with nobody near them. Every place outside of the warehouse buildings, people were at work —

unloading trucks, splitting firewood, making repairs to buildings.

Bones moved directly to the market where a pair of men holding shotguns sat on a picnic table just in front of the building's door, sipping coffee from tin cups. Above the doorway was another sign that read *"Horton's Sundries"*. The men at the table eyed the strangers as they passed. Henry stopped just short of the door and turned away, startling Shane with the unexpected movement.

The old man fished out his pipe and began packing it with tobacco from a pouch. As he packed, he took slow steps toward the seated men. "Nice place you got the makings of here," Henry said, searching his pockets for a match.

Bones shook his head and stepped away from the door. "Gus is expectin' us inside."

Henry found the match and, much to Bones' annoyance, lit the pipe, then moved to the table and sat beside the two shotgun-wielding men. "We been riding a spell, let me catch my breath a minute," Henry said, nodding to the men across from him. Shane tried to hide a grin after catching an impatient sigh from Bones. Out of habit, the soldier moved tactically behind the seated men and leaned against the building's wall.

"You got more of that coffee?" the old man asked, looking at the steaming tin cups.

One of the guards eyed Henry suspiciously, his eyes lingering over the old man's rifle before shifting his gaze to Shane. "We might," he finally grunted.

The second of the guards took a gulp of his coffee before splashing the rest to the ground. He wiped his chin with the back of his glove and looked at Henry. "If you've got questions, you should go on and speak to Gus."

"Never heard of her," Henry said before drawing in on the pipe. "Should I have?"

The first guard smiled and pressed his hands to the table as he stood. "I like your style, old man. I hope you survive 'til dinner. If you do, come look me up in the barn; I'll buy you a drink."

Bones face stiffened as he moved to the

table. "Come on, you can smoke that inside."

Henry nodded and rolled his shoulders. When Bones had turned away, he dipped his eyebrows at Shane and nodded his head. The two men followed the skinny man into the store. The door had a chime that rang as they stepped into the dark and warm interior of the building. Smelling of wood smoke and mesquite, the room was a large square, and most of the store shelves had been removed or pushed to a back wall. Along the back wall, the two men spotted gray parkas hung from a row of hooks. Where the checkout counter had been, a man now stood with a rifle; in front of him were a pair of round tables.

At the table closest to them, a group of men played cards. To the back, another pair of men sat with a third — the broad-shouldered, red-bearded man that Shane recognized as Gus. He looked up as they approached, then ushered the other two men away. He signaled a hand to the counter and the armed man behind it laid down his rifle and carried a coffee pot to the table before turning to face Henry and Shane.

"I'll take your long guns for you," the

man said.

Henry reared back and looked at the man as if he was speaking a foreign language. "I think I'll be all right," he said.

Gus cleared his throat and pointed to a rack on the wall where several rifles rested. "He ain't stealing them," he said, annoyed. "They'll be right over there and you can grab them when you leave."

Henry clenched his teeth and apprehensively stretched his arm, handing off the rifle; Shane followed and did the same. "There now; that wasn't so tough, was it?" Gus laughed, reaching for the pot and pouring the newcomers a cup of coffee. The man drew his hands back and reached for a stack of envelopes beside him. Under the envelopes was a dogeared county road atlas. "Now, about the bounties… the big ones are all but gone. All that's left are a few hold ups out on the mountain. And, well—"

"Well what?" Henry asked, blowing on the cup before taking a sip.

"I've had some men come up missing— deserters probably. I could make it worth your while if you'd be interested in tracking them down." Gus grinned, but the lines in his forehead remained hard and serious.

"It's a big country; easy for a man to disappear in. How you know these fellas ain't dead? You know, buried behind someone's barn out on the range."

The comment caught Shane off guard and caused him to spit his coffee. Gus looked up and tightened his brow. "Just who the hell are you, anyhow?"

"I reckon I'm the same as you… just a man looking to make his way. I'm Henry; this is my boy, Shane."

Gus eyed Henry and stroked his beard. "Henry and Shane, huh? You taking this cowboy shit serious, ain't ya? Rolling up on my spot all *High Plains Drifter*. Where you from, anyhow? I know it ain't north because I'd have seen you around."

"Kentucky, by way of Ohio."

"Ohio? Now, that's some tough country these days. We got boys out of there. How'd you get across the river with them horses?"

"Wasn't easy with the bridges out, but we found a barge down near Addison, used it to get on the river, rode it until we found a good spot to come ashore."

"Addison you say?" Gus looked down at the county map book and used a pen to scratch a note on the cover. "So, what brings you to Crabtree?"

Henry began to speak when Gus put up a hand. "What's with your boy here? Ain't he got a tongue?"

Shane sat back and tried to look bored. He took another sip of the coffee and looked to Gus. "Making our way to Charleston to find my brother; looking for work along the way."

"How long you plan on sticking around?"

"We heard you might have something for us. If so, once we get resupplied, we can get moving again."

Gus stared hard at Shane. The young soldier held his eye, not to be intimidated by a bully. Gus smiled and let out a loud laugh that caused others in the store to turn their heads. "Well, you heard right, boy. We got a shit load of work. So much in fact, I doubt you all will want to leave once you get elbows deep in it."

A distant explosion echoed from outside. A man near the door opened the door and looked out into the hills. On the wind carried the sounds of small arms fire. The man turned toward the far table and said, "Coming from the valley, boss."

"Who we got up there?"

The man at the door scratched his head. "A couple missing scout teams that went out clearing farms, and the mortar and machine gun crew from the ambush yesterday, but they should be back this afternoon."

The gunfire intensified before a long pause, then continued again briefly before finally stopping. Gus looked down at his hands, then back up. "Get some extra men out on those walls. If they got attacked by infected, they'll probably have some in tow when they come home."

"On it, boss," the man at the door said

before stepping out into the cold.

Gus turned his attention back to Henry. "Go with Bones, he'll get you set up in the barn; I'll call for you when I have something. Until then, have a drink on me." The man reached in his pocket and dropped a pair of .357 cartridges on the table. "That should be enough to wet your whistle."

The men got up to leave when Gus called after them. "Wait a minute. You said you heard we had work; who told you that?"

Shane gulped and glanced at Henry who'd already pulled the pipe from his mouth and was emptying it onto the hardwood floor. "Straggly kid by the name of Ricky. Bumped into him on the road headed east. Asked if I could help get him back to Columbus."

"Ricky, you say?" Gus pondered.

"Yup. He told us about your outfit. I offered to take him along, but he said he wasn't interested."

Gus turned in the direction of the two men standing off to the side. A fat chested man nodded and said, "Ricky was with the scouts; the ones sent to check out the west slope."

"And you said he was alone?" Gus asked Henry.

"Yup, all alone, walking the road, wearing a gray coat and carrying two rifles."

"Traitor, son of a bitch," the fat man grunted. "Should have known that punk would run as soon as he had a chance."

Henry cleaned the pipe with his thumb and slid it back into his breast pocket. "Ain't but a day's ride outside the gates. Sure you could catch 'em if you leave soon enough," Henry said.

Gus sighed and pointed to a man sitting at the card table. Two men got to their feet and scrambled out. Henry nodded his approval and looked back at Gus palming the .357 cartridges. "Now, you said something about a drink?"

Chapter 15

Crabtree, West Virginia
Free Virginia Territories

Gus sat watching the strangers leave the store. He snapped his fingers, calling back the men who'd been waiting in the shadows. Both were hard types and well-worn. Cousins from Indiana. They'd been with Gus since the door to door fighting in Cincinnati. He trusted them and knew them to have his back. Faces tanned and bodies calloused from living in the wild, Clyde was fat chested with a thin waist, a long scar running from his thick neck up to his cheek. Chris was gaunt, tight skinned, with bright green eyes and greasy hair. Like his cousin, he wore a pistol in a canvas shoulder holster.

The men moved to the table, and after sitting themselves, the fat one looked up at Gus. "You sure about these strangers?"

Gus hesitated, then looked across at the

fat man. "We need men, and those two seem capable."

"Yeah, but why them?" Chris asked. "They seem awful eager and cocky."

"I might'a said the same about you a year ago," Gus retorted. The cousins were wild cards when he took them in—two hungry and scared boys caught stealing from a supply wagon. Instead, he gave them a chance, where any other captain would have had them shot on the spot. It wasn't that he saw ambition, talent, or any of those admirable qualities in the cousins. It was more that he saw them as a blank slate. Two youthful men that survived the fall, living off scraps and boot heels. They'd been spared the cutthroat backstabbing that Gus had went through to reach his position. He took them under his wing because he could shape them. He reached across the table and filled his empty cup from the pot. "We're moving fast and losing men faster than we can recruit. If we want to stay on schedule, we'll need folks to go out and do the... the dirty work."

Clyde's face soured. He was a hard man, but Gus knew that Clyde was still holding on to a whimsical fantasy that he was somehow doing right by the world. That he was more than a thug. "Dirty work… I get Texas, but why is this other thing even necessary? There's plenty of country out here for us. And if word gets out, the people are going to turn on us."

Gus chuckled to himself. It was one of the drawbacks of taking in smart men; you spent as much time debating as you did getting things done. It reminded him as much of his time being a school teacher, as it did of being the captain of a rogue army. He could be hard, but he still had to take time to listen to his people or they would turn on him. There was no such thing as blind loyalty in this world; a place where any may could turn his back and attempt to make his way on his own. Gus, having done the same thing several times since the fall, knew this better than most.

"Something funny, boss?" Clyde asked, catching the man's attention.

The red-bearded man straightened his back and rose up in his chair. "Carson wants everything cleansed. The infection outside the gates wiped out. That means anyone not willing to join us has to go."

"But it's genocide," Clyde grunted. "And what about the people in that camp? We attacked them without warning; we didn't even give them a chance."

The reply came back cold and hard — even the best teacher would eventually lose his patience. "You better watch your mouth speaking like that. Carson is the only reason most of us are even alive. And with the vaccine gone and no more to be produced, this is the best chance we got at wiping out the plague. We'll save those that we can but—" He paused, searching for the right words. "This business with Cloud's people is unfortunate, I agree, but when they sided with Texas it didn't leave us many options."

The fat man hung his head and mumbled. "Texas ain't got but a dozen men this side of the Mississippi. I don't know why the General wants to go picking fights where they ain't needed."

"Today a dozen, tomorrow it could be a division of tanks from Fort Hood. It's important that we send a message," Gus said, setting his cup down hard on the table. "People need to learn that there is only one option and that's with us."

Clyde folded his hands and dipped his chin. "All I'm saying is that it's in violation of the treaty. Texas agreed to stay on their side of the Mississippi, and we agreed to protect everything on this side. Killing them farmers and preppers goes in direct conflict to what we agreed on."

"The governor's council signed that treaty, not us," Gus said, balling his hands into fists. "And you know that the Alliance was ready to turn it all over to Texas; give up everything we and Carson have worked for. We didn't stay alive this long just to give it all away. You want to go back to begging for every one of your meals?"

Chris put his hands up. "Come on now, you know it ain't like that, Gus."

Gus held his expression. He was no fool, and the other men at the table knew he was a killer when push came to shove. Chris was already reeling back in his chair, showing regret at going too far. "Carson has made the tough decisions. He made the calls that the Council was afraid to. It ain't a mystery why there's no infected left in Pennsylvania. We know what we did, and just because they don't talk about it, don't mean the people don't know it too."

Clyde bit at his upper lip. "This isn't Ohio or Pennsylvania. We're outnumbered here and as soon as the folks figure it out, we're going to be in trouble."

Gus looked across the table, studying the men's faces. "The train will be here in two days. Carson will be arriving with fresh troops and supplies. Once Crabtree is stood up and we take more places to the south, the people will see the good we can do. They'll be fed, they'll be safe, and they'll be happy. We can give this land back to the people."

"Burning camps and uprooting families isn't going to make us many friends," Clyde said.

Gus waved him off, having had enough of the discussion. He leaned back in his chair and opened the map book in front of him, flipping until he found a marked page. "The time for talking about it is over, boys. We're committed down here and we'll see it through." Gus pushed the map book to the center of the table; an overlay of the valley was marked out with several lines and areas drawn over in pen. "Best we can tell, that Ranger is still out there beating his drum for Texas. Tomorrow, I want you to take them two new boys out and see if you can find them."

"And if we find him?" Chris asked.

"Then you kill him and anyone that's with him."

Clyde pulled the map closer and moved a finger along a road. "You know, the boys said he was moving with some real soldierly types. It won't be easy."

"I trust you to figure it out." Gus's eyes glowed.

"And you trust the new fellas with this? They'll be ready to kill, just like that?"

"If they give you a reason to think off of them, then make sure they don't come back to camp."

"Just like that," Clyde said without taking his eyes off of the map.

Gus spoke softly now. "Call it a test. These boys pass, maybe we got some bigger things in store for them."

Chapter 16

Crabtree, West Virginia
Free Virginia Territories

She slept solidly, dreaming of home and a time before the war, until she was startled awake. Forcing open her eyes, she looked into the clinic. The room glowed softly from the fire of a gas lamp. Ella was standing over her, looking down with gentle eyes. "It's true, it really is you," she said, dropping to hug Chelsea's chest.

Chelsea struggled to comprehend what was happening; the events of the last days swished by in her mind like a movie. Her thoughts were blurred, but her love and emotions for Ella were real. She rubbed at her eyes, trying to focus.

Chelsea took the girl in her arms and when she pulled back, she placed her hands at the side of her cheeks pushing back her long brown hair. "Ella… how?" She looked at the girl's face; she was so much older than when she'd first met her. There were tears in the girl's eyes and her bottom lip quivered, but still she looked down and forced a smile.

Her voice came in a broken whisper. "When I heard there were more of us in the clinic, I prayed it was you. I begged them until they finally let me come and see for myself. I told them that you were my mother and I had to see you."

Chelsea held her close again before moving herself up into a seated position, swinging her legs over the side of the bed. She caught the girl eyeing the half sandwich on the tray beside her bed. "Have you eaten?" Chelsea asked her as her eyes scanned the room, confirming they were alone. Ella answered yes, but her eyes gave a different answer.

"Is Shane here?" she asked.

Chelsea closed her eyes and whispered, "I don't know… I don't know anything. Where are we?"

This time it was Ella who looked to the door to ensure they were alone. "I had to see if it was you. The nurse said you can leave. They brought you clothes."

"Leave where?" Chelsea asked, looking to a stack of folded clothing at the end of the bed. On the floor, she spotted her leather military boots, the only thing of hers that wasn't taken. Ella reached for the clothing and placed them on Chelsea's lap, then moved back to the door and closed it slightly before returning.

"Hurry, you need to get dressed," Ella whispered. "They call this place Crabtree, and they say it's a town, but it isn't. It's dirty and muddy and most of the people here live in tents."

"What people?" she asked as she went through the clothing.

"They tell us they're soldiers, but they aren't. Not like Shane or Mr. Brooks. These people are mean. They keep everyone in a barn. They told us all we have to do is be quiet and soon we will be brought to the city where everything is good."

Chelsea pulled on a ragged sweatshirt and stepped into a pair of men's denim jeans two sizes too big. "How many are here with you?"

"All the kids and most of the ladies. But none of the men are here; none of them."

Footsteps in the hallway silenced the girl. Quickly, she spun and faced the doorway with Chelsea to her back. The door swung open and the nurse stood in the doorway with a skinny, buck-toothed man close behind. The man's eyes shifted nervously between Chelsea and the girl.

The nurse smiled and opened her hands to Chelsea. "I see you've already dressed; that's good. Bones here will be showing you where you can stay until the train arrives," she said in a calming voice.

Chelsea stepped ahead and, from the corner of her eye, caught a glimpse of Ella snatching the half-eaten sandwich. She turned and faced the nurse, then squared her shoulders to look into the eyes of the man. "If you have a place to take us, then let's go." She felt Ella pull in behind her and tug at the back of her shirt.

The nurse looked at the empty plate and caught a glimpse of the sandwich in Ella's balled fist. She nodded and pursed her lips in a smile. "Of course. I know you're hungry. I know there isn't much in the lodging, but I'll ask if something more can be sent over."

"And after that?" Chelsea asked, causing the nurse to focus her eyes.

"You'll be fine, ma'am." Bones said sternly. "There'll be plenty once you get moving north and out of this hellish place."

"North where?" Chelsea asked.

Bones grew impatient and pushed the nurse aside, then swung a hand toward the doorway. "Let's go; I ain't got all night."

Chelsea stepped wearily ahead with Ella still grasping her side. Ahead of her, the hallway stretched into darkness, the only light coming from an open window at the end. Bones cleared his throat again, ushering them forward. Stepping outside, she found the night air crisp and heavy with the smell of wood smoke. She paused, allowing herself to adjust to the moonlight. The sky was filled with bright stars that appeared to hang low in the heavens. Her eyes desperately searched the camp's surroundings, but she found it dark and bathed in shadows.

She stepped farther onto the wooden porch and could see that the clinic was, in fact, a small house. The neighboring few buildings she could see had groups of armed men positioned out front, many warming themselves around steel barrels with glowing fires.

Holding a lantern in one hand and pointing to the ground with the other, Bones pushed himself around her, indicating a rough walkway made of logs and planks surrounded by overgrown grass that moved its way through the mud. She could hear men talking and the faint sounds of horses. "Watch your step, ma'am. It's just this way."

Chelsea turned on her heel and took the treads, stepping lightly onto the planks that squished against the thick mud. The walk to the side of a barn wasn't far, and soon they were stepping onto a deck plank. A pair of men armed with rifles hushed their conversation as she neared. As one man leaned back against a tall sliding door, the other, wearing a heavy wool blanket over his shoulders, approached and spit just to the front of her boots, causing her to stop. "Whatcha got for me, Bones?" he grunted.

It was too dark for her to see his face, but she had no trouble catching a whiff of the body odor and alcohol coming off of him. Bones gently nudged past her and held up the lantern, letting the glow light the man's long hard jaw and cold eyes. "Evening, Roger. It's just the girl and herma Doc was keeping an eye on. He says she's good to go now."

"So, what the hell am I supposed to do with her?" the man scoffed.

Bones hesitated then said, "Gus wants her on the train with the others."

Chelsea watched as the second man pitched forward and turned to work a lock and chain fastened to the sliding door. The other man stepped closer and looked her up and down. "I don't understand why we sending all these women up north if Carson is really intent on repopulating the south." He chuckled and shook his head at Chelsea, who painted a hard stare.

The man to the rear finished with the lock and turned back, holding the chain in his hands. He gripped the edge of the door and tugged. "Hey, Bones, you any idea how long this babysitting's going to last? Not exactly what we signed up for."

"Train'll be here day after tomorrow is all I know," Bones said. He moved an arm back, guiding Chelsea and Ella into the low light of the barn.

They stepped forward and were enveloped in the light scent of hay and the low glow of lanterns. The barn was long and wide; across from her, she looked into a row of eight stalls facing an open floor covered with straw. In the open space was a small table and chairs, and a bench with a several buckets and pitchers of water—what Chelsea guessed were toilet facilities. She was nudged forward and could see women and children cower away from the open door, avoiding eye contact with the guards. Bones opened a locked cabinet with a key and removed an old blanket and towel. He pushed them into Chelsea's hands, then pointed to the stalls on the far wall of the barn. "Find a spot to rest. There's food and water here, and you can clean up over there in the basins."

"What about a bathroom, a toilet?" Chelsea asked.

Bones grinned at her. "We'll call you for that when it's time. If you can't wait — find a bucket." The skinny man backed out of the opening and the door slid shut, locking her in. People moved, and blankets were pulled aside from the stalls as dirt-smudged faces peered out at her.

"Chelsea, is that you?" came a female voice.

Chelsea stared into the low light and took a step forward, her eyes searching for the speaker.

"Oh my god, it is you," a woman said, rushing from between hung blankets. Chelsea watched the young woman approach. She quickly recognized her from the camp. She had brilliant green eyes and chestnut hair. Karen Winters was five four, her face was thin, and her skin pale. Chelsea spoke with her often around the camp. Karen and her father went out of their way to make themselves useful, trading game and other food for work. Karen's father was a gifted craftsman and helped the camp's residents with building homes and crafting furniture.

The woman rushed forward and embraced her tight. Chelsea winced at the pain in her ribs, and the woman let go, stepping back. "You're hurt," she said, looking her up and down. "Come sit."

The woman showed her to a stool. Chelsea sat as other woman quickly hovered around her. She was given a bowl of broth and a cup of tea as she was bombarded with questions. Ella sat close by her as she quietly told them about waking up in the clinic, and just now being released with no information about what they were doing here, or who held them.

The woman explained their capture at the camp. How they'd been separated from the men, then moved to this place in trucks. They were told there were more women at the clinic, but not who or how many. Karen explained how

Ella had begged to see if her mother was among the wounded. So far, their captors had treated them well and had provided them with food, water, and shelter. Chelsea let her eyes search the barn, stopping on the doors. A double at the front and the sliding door at the back. There was a loft but the ladder had been removed.

"And we've been here three days?" she asked.

An Afghani woman nodded, and, in broken English, said, "Did they say anything of our men?"

Chelsea frowned and shook her head. "I don't know, they said we were being moved north on a train."

Karen nodded. "A man from the trucks said we were safe now. That we were being rescued and would all be relocated north where the Primals had all but been exterminated." Karen leaned forward and placed her hand on Chelsea's knee. "I have to ask—you were on watch when they attacked…"

Chelsea nodded her head slowly.

"Did you see my father?"

"No, I'm sorry. But I know our people are out there and they *will* come for us." Chelsea turned her head toward the door. From outside, they could hear men shouting, then gunfire erupted.

Chapter 17

East of Crabtree, West Virginia
Free Virginia Territories

Brooks held a finger to his lips. The point man was pressed into the foliage, nearly concealed in the shadows of overhanging brush. As a place to sleep, Brad could have wished for more comfortable accommodations. The soldier pressed in deep and slid under the boughs of a mountain pine. The men were nestled into the face of a ridge. Just ten feet below them, a snow and ice covered trail led out of the valley.

Brad could hear their plodding feet on the trail below. Turning his head, he could see them in the pale moonlight. A barefooted man walked by, dragging a bloodied stump attached to a grey and decaying leg. These were Primals; victims of the harsh winter, frozen yet still refusing to give up the ghost. Unlike humans, they didn't succumb to frost bite, get hypothermia, and die; somehow, their brains continued to function, their hearts and lungs refusing to quit until frozen solid.

It'd been months since any of them had seen a 'Creeper', as they were called. The ones that stumbled along, nearly frozen, on that last leg before finally fading to death. The Primals had evolved in the last two years; they knew to seek shelter during storms and during the frigid temperatures of winter. They hunted in packs and often — with the aid of the more intelligent Alphas — avoided danger when they could. But something was different on the mountain now… The Primals were spun up and acting irregular. The battle had stirred them, keeping the things out in the sub-freezing temperatures.

A single gunshot cracked, then echoed through the night air. The Creepers halted on the trail, then with grunting exhilaration, marched on with renewed vigilance toward the sound of the gunfire. The single gunshot became many, and soon turned to automatic weapons fire. Somewhere ahead, a one-sided battle was raging, and these things were feeding it.

For over an hour, the men of Brad's team

lay hidden in the rocks and trees, attempting sleep but shivering from the cold. Fighting the muscle cramps from holding position, until finally, the last of the Creepers had moved by. Brooks was the first to leave his hide, belly crawling to the trail below, then moving to a crouch. With his night vision covering his eyes, he searched the trail, then quickly called the others to his position. Without speaking, the team moved out rapidly into the heavy underbrush, patrolling perpendicular to the trail and keeping the sounds of the gunfire to their right.

A cold wind blew through the trees, rattling the branches and dropping snow on their heads. The sounds of the Primals' moans continued to mix with the gunfire as they trekked through the moonlit forest. Soon, Brooks turned them back to the west, toward the sounds of the raging battle. The terrain changed and they were traversing downhill. Brad slowed, checking his footing with every step as the terrain worsened; it was no time for a fall or twisted ankle. He stepped lightly, checking every step, avoiding the branches and thorns of bushes.

Just before dawn, the gunfire suddenly stopped. They descended down a stepped ledge, then turned to follow a fast running stream that snaked its way to low ground. The forest thinned, and a game trail appeared near the banks of the stream. Brooks slowed the group again and pointed out into the pink and purple predawn sky. In the distance they could see the glow of lights and campfires. Moving on, they stopped at the edge of the valley in a thick, tree line. As the sun broke, the men belly crawled the last hundred yards, reaching the last ridge overlooking a large expanse of flat ground.

Below them, Brad could see the outlines of a large timber wall, not unlike the one that surrounded the outpost he called home. Inside the wall was a farm and a grouping of buildings, not quite a village. They were close enough that Brad could see armed men moving along the tops of the walls, and men inside walking along plank boardwalks.

Looking through the optics of his rifle, Brad witnessed the results of the previous night's battle. A corpse-filled road met the fence at a large gate. The stream they'd followed continued to wend through the flat ground and pass under the wall. As the sun broke the eastern sky, he could make out tiny pillars of smoke, a large tent city, and a motor pool filled with vehicles. A train track cut right through the center of the walled compound and, looking beyond, Brad could barely identify the rise of a railroad bed that moved through the flat land.

The team was concealed in heavy trees, but there was no cover to their front; nothing but snow-covered grassland between them and the walls. Leaving Hassan to watch the compound, Brad watched as Sean pushed back away from the edge with the others following. He guided them to a small depression and into a small huddle. Sean pulled off his gloves and rubbed his fingers together. "So what do ya all think?" he said in a hushed voice.

"It's gotta be them, Chief," Cole replied. "And by the looks of those tents and the number of vehicles, there must be a lot of them."

"They dug in, built themselves up for a stay." Joey nodded in agreement. "Could be over a hundred men down there."

Brooks dropped to his rear and pushed back against a tree, then pulled a wool watch cap low over his brow. "I kinda wish we'd hauled that mortar tube along," he said, crossing his arms across his chest and closing his eyes.

Sean looked at his vest, patting the empty magazine pouches. "We don't have the ammo to hit them head-on, and if we run up against them guns blazing—we're toast."

The Ranger agreed. "This position of theirs works two ways; they got open fields of fire and so do we. We can set up here and keep them pinned inside the compound. We starve them out," Burt said.

Sean shook his head. "We don't have the time, and we don't know what other assets they've got," he said, then looking at the faces of the men around him, added, "Besides, it's not like we have loads of supplies."

Burt steeled his gaze. "Whatever; we decided Carson has to be killed."

Brooks chuckled and looked up from his nap. "Okay, tough guy. Are you even sure he's here? Do you even know what he looks like?"

The Ranger spun his head back and locked eyes with Brooks. "If he isn't here now, he will be. It's how the guy operates; he gets his kicks seeing people controlled."

Brad rolled his shoulders and nodded his head. "A guy like that should be easy enough to identify. We've all seen it before. The guy walking with body guards; the one that doesn't really fit in. The guy that's just a little too clean, with a collar shirt, surrounded by grunts." Brad grinned and gestured toward the compound with his chin. "If Carson is here, we'll find him."

A bird's call from the tree line took the men's attention back to the front. Hassan was perched behind a large rock pointing to the compound's gate. "A group of riders leaving the gate," he whispered.

Sean nodded to Hassan, then turned back into the group. "Get ready to move; and stay alert. I'm taking Brooks and Brad to gather some needed intel. The rest of you be ready to back us up."

Chapter 18

Free Virginia Territories

Breakfast was better than he'd expected. Powdered eggs and canned hash — it beat the hell out of jerky. Looking across at Henry plowing through a plate of his own, Shane watched the old man eat as he recalled how Henry had fought the night before. The gunfire started late after midnight, just as the pair had been assigned a bunk. Henry and Shane had quickly grabbed their rifles and ran to the wall to try to help. Not that they cared about this compound or its defenders, but they knew their people were being held somewhere inside.

Primals had pressed tight against the compound's gates, attempting to get inside. Guards ran along the tops of the fences, then tossed oil-soaked torches to the ground to the right of the gate in a section of the wall that was heavily reinforced with earth. The Creepers took the bait, drawn toward the fire and away from the weaker gates. Shane fired directly down into the heads of the infected, the Winchester proving accurate and deadly. Beside him, Henry — with a steady hand and unshakable resolve — racked his own rifle, rapidly firing into the mob, not wasting a round.

When the size of the mass doubled, and then tripled in size, Shane watched as machine guns were removed from the backs of trucks and brought to the perimeter. As more guards reported to the fence, Shane was pushed to the back and soon ordered to return to his quarters. With everyone focused on the fight, Henry and Shane found themselves alone; they decided to wander close to the barn. With it so closely guarded — three men to every door — they didn't speak in order to avoid drawing attention to themselves. Light shone through the planks, and shadows moved across the cracks. It was very apparent something important was being kept inside.

"Watcha thinking about?" Henry asked,

sliding his cleaned plate away and breaking Shane's daydream.

Shane let his eyes wander the mess hall. It was in an old, three-car garage, long and wide, with block walls and a cement floor. The building was surprisingly warm, thanks to a woodstove in each corner. Seeing that nobody cared or bothered to observe him, he turned back to Henry. "These guys are better than they look," he whispered. "I'm worried."

Henry nodded, taking a gulp from a cup of coffee and letting his eyes inspect the other men in the makeshift mess hall. "Ain't none of 'em look like military, but they sure is organized like it. And that call to the wall last night was disciplined; it's something they've practiced."

Shane leaned in close, speaking low to ensure nobody would hear. "And the barn," he said.

"Yup, I noticed that. It's the only place big enough to hold your people." Henry scoffed. "But we can't get in."

Shane looked up and noticed two men enter the mess hall with Bones. He recognized the two from the previous day's meeting with Gus. The men's heads panned, searching the faces in the mess hall until Bones locked on his gaze. He raised a hand, throwing a friendly wave, and swiftly approached.

"Here they are," Bones said, moving to the head of the table. "How'd you boys sleep last night?"

Shane nodded and tried to look uninterested as Henry stretched and yawned. "Like a newborn. We appreciate the digs; sure as hell beats the trail."

Bones smiled and turned, pointing to the men standing beside him. "Want to introduce ya'll to some folks. This here is Chris and Clyde." Shane looked the men over, seeing right off that they both carried pistols in shoulder rigs. The first impression they gave off was that they were in charge.

The bigger of the two, Clyde, put a hand on Bones' shoulder and ushered him away. The fat man moved to the table and dropped into an empty seat. The other man circled around and stood just behind Shane; he seemed to stand intentionally close, as to draw discomfort. Clyde reached into a shirt pocket, pulled out a cigarette, and waved it at Henry. Henry shrugged and the fat man lit a match.

"Got some work for you two," the fat man said, fumbling to light the cigarette.

"Yeah, that's what we came here for," Henry grunted.

Clyde grinned. With the cigarette hanging from his mouth, he exhaled through his nose. He reached into a cargo pocket on his pants and dumped a box of 30-30 shells onto the table. "Boys said you helped out on the wall last night. This ought to cover your expenses."

Henry reached for the box and opened it up. "It'll do. We intend to earn our keep."

"Good—I like to hear that," Clyde said. "Too many boys these days are just along for the board and three squares. We need more go getters like ya'll seem to be."

Henry laughed. "Well, don't go getting attached; come spring, we're back on the trail."

"I get that, but time being we could use

your help," Clyde said, holding back a grin. The fat man pushed back from the table and rose to his feet. "Get your gear and meet us out front in twenty. We've got a patrol missing. Gus wants us to take a ride and see if we can't locate 'em."

"A patrol? That sounds easy enough. What were they doing out there?" Shane asked.

The cousins looked at each other, then at Shane, eyeing him suspiciously. Finally the fat man nodded and Chris spoke up. "We had some trouble with a group a few days ago. After we dealt with most of them, we had the patrol stay back to search for survivors."

"Survivors?" Shane said, frowning.

"Yeah, this group. They were holding a number of women and children captive. We were able to free most of them. But we suspect there were more of the captors out there."

"So, you left a group behind to make sure nobody followed you back to Crabtree?" Shane said, gesturing to the room.

"Well, specifically speaking, you got it about right, but we don't suspect any trouble."

"This trouble… if you aren't expecting more of it—then where are your missing men?" Shane asked, now turning his head to look Clyde in the eye.

He felt Chris behind him; the man gripped the back of Shane's chair, intentionally pressing his knuckles into Shane's back. "The kid asks a lot of questions," the man said.

Henry waved a hand. "Hey, you don't stay alive this long not knowing what the hell you're getting into. We're just making sure."

Clyde shrugged, laughing. "I think we're going to be all right," the fat man said sarcastically. "Get your horses and meet us outside in twenty," he concluded, walking away.

***

They rode away from the compound single file. The two Raiders dressed in the familiar gray parkas. Chris in the front and Clyde in the back, they moved slowly down the blacktop road.

With the high ground of the mountain valley to their right and open prairie to the left, the only sound was that of the clop of horse hooves. Shane didn't dare look behind him, but he was sure if he had, he would find a barrel pointed at his back. Henry was just ahead of him, riding close to Chris; at every opportunity, the old man would try to spark a conversation with the lead man. Every time, the attempt was met with Chris increasing his pace to create distance.

Shane tried to steady himself and hide his inexperience as a horseman from the cousins. After a short distance, he realized most of his concern was unneeded, as the cousins appeared to have even less experience than him. Henry rode easy, letting the reins lay across his lap. With his hands tucked away in his jacket pocket, he looked as if wouldn't be any more comfortable on an old recliner. The old man made a clicking sound with his mouth and rushed his horse ahead and abreast of Chris. "You've got a good animal there; how long you had him?" Henry asked.

Chris appeared to be tense in the saddle and was hesitant at make any changes to the horse's gait. He rode stiff-backed and uncomfortable. "It's not my horse. I don't know shit about it, so don't bother asking," Chis spat back.

Henry's reply was terse. "Damn, son, didn't mean to piss in your pocket."

Chris pulled up on the rein to stop, and turned in the saddle to face Henry. "Now, just what the hell is that supposed to mean?"

The old man shrugged confusion and looked back to Clyde. The thick-necked cousin grinned. "Settle down, Chris. Save it for the other guys."

Before Chris could argue, Henry put up his gloved hand and reeled his horse back. The riders stopped as Henry dismounted his horse and quickly stepped to the shoulder of the road. He leaned forward with a hand over his eyes, shielding them from the morning sun. Clyde grunted and rode up alongside the old man, now drawing his rifle from the scabbard. "Something bothering you, old timer?" he said.

Henry moved his jaw like chewing a piece of leather, then spit on the ground. "Something's up there," he said, moving his head into the direction of the high ground that flanked the blacktop road.

"It's nothing," Chris mocked.

Shane maneuvered his horse around Chris, flanking the other men. He let his gun hand rest on the butt of his pistol as his eyes focused up in the trees. The steep hill to the south moved up at a sharp angle away from the road. The crest was lined with thick trees shadowed by the sun coming up in the west. Shane followed the hill to where it was notched out, knowing it was the spot where the road intersected with the valley trail they'd followed a day earlier.

"Naww," Henry muttered. "I saw a glimmer when we first started out, thought it was nothing, but I just seen it again."

Chris paused and shook his head before kicking his horse. "It's just the snow and ice reflecting off the sun. You're seeing things, old man."

Clyde nodded in agreement and followed his cousin. Henry took another long glance at the tree line before climbing back into his saddle to follow the others. Shane rode up and fell abreast of the older man. "What do you think it was?" he asked in a low voice.

Henry shook his head, digging for his pipe. "Can't be certain, maybe the kid's right and it's just ice," he said, watching the younger men ride away. Henry removed his gloves and trotted his horse back to the center of the street. He pulled the pipe and started his routine of packing tobacco. He dipped his head and used his hands to shield the pipe from the wind as he lit it.

Looking up again, he made sure the cousins were out of earshot, then lowered his voice. "Somebody is out there."

Shane's head pivoted side to side.

"Somebody that don't want these boys to see them," Henry said.

Chapter 19

Brad sprinted through the tree line, dropping to a slide along the shoulder of a snow swept road. He knew Sean and Brooks were ahead of him, closer to the intersection and positioned higher on the slope. He stashed his rifle and pack in the snow, pushed his sidearm into his waist, and pulled the bloodied, gray parka over his head.

He staggered toward the center of the road, just catching sight of horsemen rounding the corner. Brad moved into the deeper snow and dropped to his knees as he raised a hand. He crawled forward and watched as the lead rider pulled up on the reins, stopping his horse. He waved his hand up and down crawling forward, carefully eyeing the lead horsemen. The man raised a rifle and leveled it in Brad's direction, but didn't fire.

Brad took another stumbling step, then collapsed into the snow. He belly slid forward before rolling to his back, letting his arms drop to the snow. He could hear the men now, shouting to each other, but unable to make out the words. The horses clopped forward, he could hear their heavy breathing as the snorted into the cold air.

"He bit?" he heard a rider call out.

"How the hell should I know?" another responded.

"Well, he's got one of our jackets; go check him out."

"I ain't touching him! He might be infected. Have the kid go do it; that's what we're paying him for, right?"

Brad fought the temptation to turn his head or reach for his pistol. He had to trust that Sean and Brooks would put the riders in the ground before any could do him harm. He heard a horse stomp and the creak of a saddle as a man's boots hit the ground. He caught a glimpse of a square-shouldered man pass him by. The sun shone in his eyes, preventing him from making out details, but not keeping him from seeing the pistol in the man's hand. The figure stepped closer, the sun blocking his face. The man knelt over his body, reared back, then leaned in close and whispered, "Brad, is that you?"

Brad turned his head and looked directly into the eyes of Shane. "Ahh, hell," he said.

"What?" Shane asked, confusion in his voice.

"Listen, I don't have time to explain, but you need to get your hands in the air now."

Shane's eyes grew wide with recognition. He wasn't too stupid not to recognize an ambush when he saw one. Brad rolled hard in the snow and pulled his pistol. He launched to his feet and planted the barrel under Shane's chin, causing the man to lose balance. Brad spun the man around, his left hand gripping his neck as his right extended the pistol toward the men on horseback.

Shane flinched then dropped the pistol and straightened his arms. "Take it easy, Brad. We're still on the same side, right?"

Brad kept aim at the lead horseman who was now leveling a rifle at him. The man's horse, feeling the tension in the air, was turning and backing away. "What am I dealing with here, Shane?" Brad said in a low voice. "You gotta help me out before lead starts flying."

Shane dipped his head to his chest and mumbled, "The old man is with me; the other two are part of the camp's raiders."

"And what are you doing with them?" Brad asked, seeing that the lead rider had now taken control of his mount. A skinny-faced man in a gray parka slowly trotted toward him with his rifle held high.

Not waiting for an answer, Brad pointed the pistol back at Shane. "Don't come any closer, mister. I won't hesitate to kill him."

The skinny-faced man smiled. "I think we have a misunderstanding. I couldn't give two shits about that boy your holding. All I'm wonder is if this good ole 44-40 round will tear through both of ya." The man put the lever action rifle to his shoulder and smiled.

Brad squeezed the pistol in his grip. There

were two riders besides Skinny Face. The old man was sitting back with one hand in his jacket pocket, the other holding the reins of Shane's horse. The third, with a bear's chest and thick neck, had a hand on the grip of a holstered pistol, but as yet hadn't drawn it. Skinny Face was still over fifty feet off; a long shot with a pistol and even if he managed to drop the first man, the others would be able to draw down on him.

"I'm giving you a count of three to drop your pistol," Skinny Face said, locking back a hammer on the rifle. Before Brad could make a final decision to fire or surrender, the riders head exploded in a pink mist — moments later, the report of a rifle echoed all around them. The body slumped to the side and fell to the road.

Brad shifted his point of aim to the third rider, the man now sitting stone cold under the sudden realization that the stranger they'd just rode up on was not alone. Brad released Shane from his grip. "Pick up your pistol, Shane. And if that old man is a friend of yours, tell him to get his hands up before Brooks pops his grape."

The old man heard the command and

lifted his hands. "I don't want any trouble, mister."

Bear chest puckered his brow but remained frozen, his hand still on the pistol grip. His eyes were locked on the road where the dead man lay. "Come on, Clyde, just do as he says," the old man called out.

The big man lolled back, his hand still resting on the gun. His head shifting from Shane to Brad and back again as he looked them each in the eye. Brad watched the big man's jaw quiver. "Better listen to him. You don't have to die here," Brad said, keeping his weapon pointed.

Clyde's hand lifted slightly from the grip of the pistol. He pumped his hand, flexing his fingers, his eyes now fixed on Brad. Out of the high ground, the team emerged. Hassan, Cole, Joey, and Burt moved swiftly out of the trees toward the road. Brad knew the SEALS would still be behind the glass until the last man surrendered, or was put down. Without sparing time for discussion, Cole ran directly to Clyde and, grabbing him by the gun hand, pulled him from the horse. The man hit the snow-covered road with a thump.

While Cole and Burt restrained Clyde, the other two turned their attention to Henry. The old man still had his hands in the air. Shane yelled, stopping their assault. "He's friendly, fellas," he said.

Henry smiled. Still showing his palms, he lowered himself from his horse and lifted his jacket so the soldiers around him could see his sidearm.

Hassan moved in and circled the man before touching a hand to the horses back. "Is this the man that carried you from the valley?" he asked, looking at Shane.

Shane nodded. "Yes; if it wasn't for Henry, I'd be dead."

"Ya'll are dead anyway. My people know we're out here; they'll come after us!" Clyde yelled. "Double crossing sons a bitches," he said, struggling against Cole, who was stuffing a rag into the man's mouth. They then lifted and strapped him over the horse's saddle; all the while, the man kicking and fighting against the restraints.

Brad looked up to see the SEALs moving down the hill. Sean was pumping his fist and yelling for them to move out. The snipers joined the group with Brooks, who was keeping his rifle in the direction of the camp. "We need to move, boss, I don't like being in the open like this."

Sean shouted in Brad's direction, "Come on, move us out."

"Where the hell are we going?" Brad rebutted.

Henry, now back on his horse, rode close. "I know a place."

Sean looked at the man, then to Shane, who nodded. "He's okay."

"All right, then get us to this place of yours," Sean barked.

Henry looked at the soldiers, then back to the horse. "We got four mounts and ten men."

"You're good with numbers," Sean spat. He pointed at Brad. "Take two of the others and ride ahead; we'll follow along and make sure we don't pick up a tail."

Brad pointed to Cole and Hassan, then nodded before approaching the dead man's horse. He placed a boot in the stirrup and swung into the saddle; Cole climbed up behind him while Hassan rode with Shane. Henry attached a lead rope to Clyde's horse, then moved them off the road and into the flat terrain. He turned back to Sean. "It's less than file miles from here, just follow the railroad tracks. There's a cutoff that leads to a friend's place; it's where the grass turns to woods."

"I got it," Sean said.

The old man's horse whinnied as he turned it around. Henry gave the reins a tug and a snap, driving the horse into the packed snow. The ground was frozen, so the horses had good footing moving over the thick grass. Brad rode stiffly with Cole behind him, up and over the railroad bed, then down into a small gulch that couldn't be seen from the road.

***

The prairie turned to forest. Henry led on and vanished into a sharp turn that soon became a narrow path. Brad followed close behind

Clyde's horse, watching the man occasionally struggle against his bindings. The trail twisted into a ravine then dropped again down a slope. At the bottom, Henry pulled up and dismounted the horse. He stepped just into the trees, then put a hand up. "Something's wrong," he said, pulling his rifle from the scabbard.

The other men quickly followed suit, dismounting and moving to Henry's position before spreading out and taking security. "What is it?" Brad asked.

The old man extended the lever action rifle with one hand, pointing deep into the darkness of the forest. "Out there is Montague's cabin."

Brad shook his head. Looking through the woods, he could faintly pick up a clearing filled with yellow grass and snow, beyond it an old slide of mud and sedimentary rocks. He squinted and scanned again, there was no house. "I don't see it."

Henry retrieved a pipe from his pocket and began packing it with tobacco. "Yeah, you ain't supposed to. But what do you see between us and that meadow out yonder? Look at the trees instead of the forest. What does it tell you?"

Brad stepped into the tree line as he'd seen Henry do. This time, instead of looking to the end, he started close and gradually scanned outward. His eyes locked on several blackened stumps and downed trees. Farther out was a thick oak, pock-marked with bullet holes; focusing, he saw several more with the same scars. "They've been here. There was a fight," he said, just to hear his own voice. He looked behind him and caught the recognition of his men.

Henry lit the pipe and walked his horse to a tree before tying it off. "T'was afraid of this. I caught a few of them raiders up at my place awhile back." He turned and pressed the stock of his rifle into Clyde's ribs, causing the bound man to grunt. "There isn't but a handful of folks like me that live in this line on the valley." He puffed on the pipe then put the tip into the corner of his mouth. "One was old Dan Cloud. Now, I hear Dan is doing just fine on his side of the holler, so that just leaves Montague."

"And Montague is here?" Brad asked, his

eyes still on the meadow.

"I reckon," Henry said. He met Brad's eyes, then finally looked down at his boots before speaking again. "Leave your men here with the horses. I'll walk you and Shane up to check things out."

"I'd prefer we stick together," Brad said.

The old man grinned. "I'd prefer you all stay in one piece. Montague has the approach booby-trapped. I can walk you all through, but I don't trust the horses on the path. And besides, you really want your friends following us into a minefield?"

Brad nodded and pointed back to Cole and Hassan. "You all keep your eyes open."

"Once we get into Monty's place and your friends show up, I'll come back out and take you and the horses around the long way."

"Is that it?" Brad asked.

"No, that isn't it—Monty isn't keen to visitors. And by the looks of the place, he might be itching for a fight, so stay close," Henry said.

The old man didn't allow for a response; instead, he moved into the trees and walked directly toward a tall oak. From there, he made a fist and put it to his eyes. Looking through it like a telescope, he seemed to focus on a far-off object. He then extended his arm straight out. "It's this way," he said, moving out.

Shane and Brad followed, staying close as they were told. "This Montague — Monty — you say he has mines in here?"

"Yeah, that's right. He planted them in and around these trees. That's why you see the stumps; someone triggered them recently."

"Could it be animals?" Brad asked. "Like a deer."

Henry paused and pointed to signs of a fight. Bloody drag trails and spent rifle cartridges. Swinging his arm closer to the meadow, there were frozen bodies in twisted poses. Brad gulped and stepped lightly, following the old man down a straight line that led directly through the trees and into the meadow. At the end of the path, Henry walked into the grass and finally sat on a huge stone boulder. He tapped the pipe against the stone, clearing it and placed it back into his pocket.

Brad moved beside the old man and searched the meadow. He grinned when he saw it. At the end of what looked like a flat face of a stone wall was an opening. He pointed. "Monty's house is in there?" he asked.

Henry nodded but didn't speak. Shane moved up beside him and put a hand on his shoulder. "Something wrong?"

"Monty wouldn't let anyone get this close to the place without greeting them with a scatter gun," he said, getting back to his feet. He checked the action on his rifle then stepped off again, leading the way.

Brad and Shane spaced out, bringing their rifles up and moving tactically behind the sauntering old man. As they moved closer to the rock face, Brad could make out the shapes of a flagstone path and then a driveway. The rock face turned out to be nothing more than an earthen berm, carefully stacked with tall rocks to make it look natural. Beyond it was a large yard with a driveway cutting through it. At the end of the drive was a smaller fence made of dry-stacked fieldstone. There was a steel gate that opened up to a large, red-stained cabin with a two-car attached garage.

Henry paused again near the gate and pointed to snow-covered bodies in the yard. "There was a fight here. I can see that Monty did his share of the killing," he said. Henry turned around and pointed back to the tall berm. "He had dugouts up there. Places where he'd sit and do some deer and turkey hunting. He's also got CCTV wires running underground." He pointed to the cabins roof. "Entirely made up of solar panels. Only one like it out here."

"Was he alone?" Brad asked.

The old man frowned and nodded. "He done everything right; built a place out here, got his family home when the infections first hit the news. It just wasn't enough." Henry sighed and turned away before continuing. "His boys disappeared out on a hunt one morning. We looked far and wide but never found a trace of 'em. Sickness took his wife last winter. Yeah... just like me, he was alone."

Henry continued up to the house, stepping over another dead man where the driveway met a second flagstone path. He wended around trees and shrubs to a steel door fastened into the side of the garage. The door was closed and secured, but a long streak of blood was on the surface and knob. Henry put a gloved hand to the door and found it locked. He side-stepped and pulled back a bit of cedar siding, revealing a small, gray box. He opened it and removed a key. The key fit and the door clunked open.

Moving inside, Brad detected the pungent smell of death in the air. The garage floor was stacked with boxes and split firewood. Only one vehicle—an old C-10 pickup truck—sat inside, the truck bed loaded with canvas sacks. Henry caught Brad looking at the truck. "Monty collected surplus military gear; lots of it before things fell apart."

Brad nodded his understanding. Henry pointed at the concrete floor. Dark stains led a path to an open door leading into the house. The old man rolled his shoulders and let out a deep knowing sigh. He followed the blood trail through the garage to the door and into the cabin. The door opened into a modern kitchen lit by sky lights. On a granite counter top was a bloody, olive green army jacket and pair scissors. As they stepped closer, Henry stopped and looked down. Brad moved up beside them, and they found Monty.

Sitting on the floor in front of the kitchen sink with his legs straight out in front of him. The old man's head was slumped down. His left hand tightly gripped a bloodied fighting knife with a curved blade. His right hand clenched against the bloody bandages on his abdomen. His brown T-shirt was torn and cutaway, revealing wounds and gauze stuck to the old man's chest. Beside him was a Saiga-12 shotgun and a bandoleer of magazines. An open first aid kit was spilled across the kitchen floor. Henry bit at his lower lip; he turned to retrieve the army jacket and draped it over his friend's head.

"Just like Monty — he wasn't one to quit. He stopped them from taking his place, but they still kil't him," Henry said. He stood back and nodded his head with his eyes closed. "You stopped 'em, Monty, and I can't help but think if you hadn't, these men would have come for me next. Instead of three, I'd have faced ten," he whispered.

Brad backed away, giving Henry his space. He turned to survey the house. All of the windows were covered with heavy drapes. They'd stepped into the kitchen, which opened into a great room containing a few chairs and a sofa, a number of work benches, and, in the corner, a CB radio. At the back of the room was a staircase. Brad took slow steps toward the radio and, getting closer, he could see a small, flat-panel display. A green light was lit at the corner of the panel; Brad tapped a mouse and the screen flickered to life.

As Henry said earlier, the entire property was covered with cameras. A square in the center of the display was flashing motion. Brad clicked on the box and an image of his men waiting by the horses enlarged to the center of the big screen.

"Monty made his money in private security," Henry said, startling Brad.

Brad turned, looking at the richly

decorated house. "What kind of security?"

The old man smiled and pushed on a panel in the wall, revealing a small key ring. Henry caught the suspicious glance from Brad. "After Monty lost his wife, he showed me where everything was kept and how it all worked. I did the same for him up at my place." Henry held the key in his hand and led Brad through the house to what looked like the entry to a bedroom.

The key turned easily and the door opened. Inside were shelves of ammunition, food, and camping gear. Brad walked through the room, marveling at the items. "Why did he have all of this?"

Henry laughed. "He claimed most of this stuff was left over from his business days. He did a lot of contracting work outside the country. He helped train and setup security on construction sites overseas." Henry looked around the room. "He always denied it, but I know he was one of those survivalists; people with money don't hide on the back side of a mountain."

Brad pushed aside an ammo can and pulled at a large box before opening it; inside were olive drab uniforms that matched the army jacket found on the kitchen counter. He took one out and held it up. Henry shook his head. "I always asked why he hung onto those. He said that one day people will rebuild and nothing brings folks together like a uniform." Henry walked out of the room and turned back. He pointed to the security monitor. "Looks like your friends are here. I'll go fetch them."

Chapter 20

Chelsea was from upstate New York and still she had never been on or visited a farm. She'd certainly never been in a barn used as a prison. What she didn't know about barns, she made up for with her knowledge of mechanics and leadership. Looking at the building's structure, she was sure she could find a way out of the makeshift jail. But she couldn't escape alone; she would need the help of the other women. As soon as she'd arrived, she'd begun organizing them into teams to help her. Lookouts, planners, Intel gathers. She was determined that she would escape and bring back help.

Karen and another young woman had been sent for by the guards and allowed to leave the barn to work with the kitchen staff on several occasions. The two women were able to gather needed information. The nurse in the clinic hadn't lied to Chelsea; the people of Crabtree did see the women as survivors and a commodity to the settlements in the North. The fighting and survival of the fittest nature of the virus left most of the northern cities in a high male to female ratio.

The group of women at Crabtree were destined to be moved north and eventually resettled in Pennsylvania. This was a process that had already taken place several times over the last year. Raiding parties would move south. The raiders would root out hostiles, eradicate the infected, and rescue any survivors. Once a beach head was established in the new territory, a train would roll into a secured fort, delivering more men and resources. Then survivors, as they were called, would be brought onto the train and returned to the North.

Crabtree was situated around a north-south, east-west intersection. From above, the buildings were laid out in the shape of a cross with the barn positioned in the south-west quadrant. Around the buildings, the community was completely encircled in an earthen and log berm. The barn was under constant guard, but only the entrances were watched, and at night, much of the barn was concealed in darkness. The lack of light and the fact that the back of the barn was close to one of the berms gave them an advantage. The women had already begun the task of loosening boards and planks from the back corner so that she could make her escape.

Lying alone in one of the livestock stalls, Chelsea lay awake, looking at the ceiling above her. She could hear the false conversations and laughter near the main door, which was used to cover the sounds of the women working on the planks. In her hand, she held an eight-inch spike—a long, flat-headed nail removed from the barn's flooring. Most of the women possessed one now, and it would be their only weapon if the captors tried anything against them.

She debated if she was doing the right thing. Maybe it was best if she sent one of the healthier women. There were others that were just as capable of reaching Dan Cloud or the outpost. But she couldn't face the idea of one of them being in extreme danger, or facing a Primal armed only with floor spikes; she had to go herself. She knew the terrain and could get there quickly. Even with her injuries, she was certain she could find the outpost. But would the guards shoot her? She had to expect to be shot at. She sat up in the cot, feeling the crippling pain in her ribs. She winced and pushed it to the back of her thoughts.

She could tolerate the pain; it was only for a short sprint, Chelsea told herself. She would get through the barn, up and over the wall, and then make a mad dash to the cover of the forest. Once there, she could rest and disappear into the mountain. She would be able to take her time and nurse her injuries.

Chelsea sat up and rubbed the spike in her hand. She put on her boots and layered her clothing. Ella pulled back the curtain and embraced her. "Don't go, Chelsea," she whispered. "Shane will come."

Chelsea swallowed and looked away. She hadn't told Ella about the battle and how she'd lost track of Shane, and that she didn't know if he was alive. She took the girl in her arms, holding her until other women entered the stall.

Karen stepped ahead. She could see the discomfort in Chelsea's face. "I can do this," she said. "I know the mountain as well as you do, and Cole will be looking out for me. I know he will."

Chelsea forced a smile and took the woman's hand. "No, I can't ask you to do that," she said.

Before Karen could answer, they heard the sound of a train's whistle. The ground rumbled and the men outside began to hoot and cheer. "Oh no, we're too late," a woman gasped.

There was a rattle of chains at the door and it slid open, letting in a bright light. The compound was alive with trucks starting and men running along the boardwalk with rifles. Bones stepped into the opening with a wide smile. "Well, it's your lucky day, ladies! Carson has arrived," he proclaimed. "Now, get your belongings and form a single file line; he'll be eager to meet ya," Bones shouted as men rushed into the barn from behind him.

They were quickly bunched together. Men gathering their meager items into bundles of blankets and sheets and shoving them into their arms. Chelsea stumbled forward, keeping Ella tight to her body. She curled her wrist, tucking the spike into the sleeve of her shirt. Men rushed around them, so many that an attack would be certain to fail. The men instilled chaos that was designed to confuse and disorient the prisoners. They were pushed together like cattle, then led out of the barn and onto the boardwalk.

Forced into the cold night air, Chelsea looked up. Through the frozen mist, she could see that the railroad gate was open. A bright light shone though as the train approached, blowing its whistle. The women were guided forward, then pushed ahead and formed into a long line standing shoulder to shoulder. The diesel-electric locomotive moved into view, pulling freight cars. Its breaks squeaked as its engine roared. The train stopped and the gates were closed behind it.

Her legs shook from the cold and she felt the trembling hand of Ella on her hip. More men stepped to the train, cheering as doors opened on the passenger cars; armed men spilling out into the yard, those outside slapping greetings. The celebrations hushed as a large man with a black watch cap and red beard came into view. He walked the boardwalk from a building across the street. He moved to Bones' side on a flat, plank deck, exchanging words before looking to the women with a broad, toothy smile. Bones pointed to one of the barn guards, who then turned toward the line.

A light flashed in her face as a man with a scarred brow inspected her from head to toe. He grunted approval and cold hands grasped her arms and dragged her from the line. Ella resisted, not letting go until Chelsea looked down at her. "It's okay, Ella," she said, looking back to see Karen drawing the girl to her side. More women were grabbed and removed from the line, then led to the plank deck. Chelsea followed the others with her head down, avoiding eye contact.

She was moved along the back of the deck then turned around, facing away from the train. At the opposite side, Bones stood next to the red-bearded man. The man dismissed Bones with a wave of his hand, then leered at the group of prisoners. "Settle down, ladies, I know you're all excited to be heading home," he said, stepping forward. "You all can call me Gus, and as soon Mr. Carson makes his rounds, we'll get you all boarded and on your way." He said it as if he were a conductor.

Chelsea leaned out and looked left and right from the corners of her eyes. She'd been separated from the others along with eight to ten other women of similar build and height. Her eyes wandered, spotting men in a guard tower over the wall. More men lined the tops of the fence, all of them looking on excitedly at the spectacle below. She relaxed her arm, letting it hang close to her side, and felt the spike still tucked into the cuff of her shirt. Her legs shook and she took deep breaths, closing her eyes and forcing away the fear. Boots slapped in the mud behind her and she heard a baritone voice greeting men as he was led in Chelsea's direction.

A tall, powerfully-built man walked along the boardwalk then stepped onto the deck. He walked close to Gus, ignoring the women on display. He exchanged a handshake, then shifted his eyes along the deck. He looked back at Gus. "Where is Carl?"

Gus kept his eyes fixed. "Sorry, sir, your son is out on patrol. We tried to persuade him to stay back, but he insisted on leading several of the patrols himself."

"Really?" Carson said, his expression unchanged. "Carl? Leading?"

"Yes, sir," Gus bluffed. "Carl has been a real asset."

Carson smiled and turned to face the women, clapping his hands together. "So now, what have we got here?" he said proudly before stepping closer.

Carson pivoted on the heels of his boots and moved to the end of the line. He began asking questions that Chelsea couldn't hear. A woman mumbled a response and the big man laughed. He shifted down a position, now two places away from Chelsea. She flexed her wrist and let the flat head of the spike drop into her palm. Her hands were sweating despite the cold, but her mind was focused; she looked straight into the darkness, focusing on the task at hand.

She was determined she wouldn't go; she wouldn't board the train. She would drive the spike through Carson's neck and end all of this tonight. She blocked any internal debate about consequences and what they would do to her. What would happen to the women if she succeeded? She didn't care. This was the man that ordered the attack against her home and killed her friends.

She heard him laugh as he asked questions of the woman to her right. He turned and took another step, stopping directly in front of her. The man was tall; her eyes rested just below his squared chin. He bent his legs mockingly, squatting to her level, and looked her in the eyes.

He smiled and licked his teeth. "Now, what's got you so upset?"

Pyrotechnic pops from somewhere in the distance turned the man's head. The sky above the camp was suddenly illuminated with red and white flares. Chelsea smiled, knowing that help had finally arrived. With her eyes focused on the pulsing carotid artery of the man's neck, she swung the spike forward.

Chapter 21

Crabtree, West Virginia
Free Virginia Territories

The women picked up on the big man's mannerisms toward Gus. They knew he was one not to be toyed with. Gus held back placing himself on the edge of the deck, giving Carson room to make his customary inspection. He took no pleasure from this exercise, but since the fall, his life had become about survival, and this was a part of it. Carson stood a little straighter and approached the line.

Gus hated this part, the transfer of people from the field to the train destined to parts unknown for resettlement. Even though he was responsible for the prisoners being there, he tried to think of it as just another job, but seeing their faces lined up like cattle reminded him of his place in all of it. This was a larger group than usual; rarely had they found so many people living successfully below the Ohio River. Most survivors had made their way to the safe zones in Michigan by now. Only fools remained in the dead lands. He watched Carson walk among them, examining them like stock, as he'd watched the man do plenty of times before.

The only way Carson got to his position in life was for others to back down. Carson knew it, and most of those close to him knew that. He made a point of forcing people into submission, and that's what this entire display was all about. Just the sight of Carson put the women's eyes down to the deck through intimidation. He stood close, invading their personal space to instill fear with his presence; bullying them, and assessing their level of cooperation. His eyes wandered over them, pausing several times as he asked pointed questions. Ten women had been pulled from the group; a *sampling*, Carson called it. He would address them, put fear and respect into their hearts, then return them to the group to spread his message.

Carson walked along the line of prisoners, stopping at the end. Speaking with them one at a time, he planted bits of poison into their minds before moving to the next in line. The women were afraid. Avoiding eye contact, their voices broke when speaking. Carson sidestepped one at a time, stopping to face each one before asking casual questions and awaiting a response.

Gus, standing to the rear, let his eyes move right along the line while performing his own brand of inspection. He stopped and settled on a woman in the middle. She was different from the others; small boned and of average height, her hair was pulled back and her eyes were frozen on a spot far into the distance. Unlike the others who slouched and cowered, this woman stood like a soldier at attention, her hands balled into fists. She had a look of defiance; she was dangerous.

Carson pivoted and stopped directly to the front of the strange woman. He looked her up and down and laughed, trying to break her. The woman's head remained frozen and unmoving. Carson squatted mockingly to bring himself to her height.

Distant pops and explosions sounded, and suddenly the sky above them was lit in red glows. Gus, scanning the woman's hands, suddenly realized the danger and acted on reflex without thinking. Instantly, a long-rusted spike appeared in the woman's grip. She lunged forward. The spike, intended for Carson's throat, was instead deflected by Gus's left forearm.

His right hand came around and swatted the defiant woman to the wooden deck, the spike stuck inches deep in his arm. The other women screamed and scattered. Distracted by the exploding flares and now the low roar of the infected, many of the guards had missed the attack. Gus reached down and lifted the woman by the back of her neck. She fought against him, digging her nails into his forearms. He pulled the spike from his arm and placed the rusty tip just inches from the woman's eye. He swung her around and locked her into a tight choke hold. She continued to kick as he looked to Carson for a response. His leader stared at the gasping woman and smiled.

Men ran to the parapets, searching for the source as more flares were launched. Ignoring the action around him, Carson straightened his jacket and stepped close, snarling and putting his face inches from the woman's. "Get them boarded, and make sure this one is secured in my car. If you can't get this under control," he said, pointing to the sky, "we will be leaving,"

Gus nodded and pulled the woman away, relaying the order just as automatic gunfire erupted at the main gate of the camp. Men on the parapet and in the towers tumbled back, hit by heavy machine gun fire. Gus turned and shoved the woman at Bones. "Get them loaded. I want this attack put down," he shouted. The red-bearded man drew his pistol and moved to the main tower to direct the fight.

Attacked all along the front, his men were falling. He rallied fighters running from the tent city and directed them to the compound's perimeter. The majority of his force were on the eastern wall; only a handful were manning the back gate to the west, and most of the north and south walls were completely unmanned but for a few scouts. He needed a vantage point to direct the defense. He marched directly to the tower located to the right of the east railroad gate. Once there, he reached for the ladder and pulled himself to the top.

Two guards lay dead on the tower floor;

the low walls — splintered and smacked with enemy gun fire — were testimony to how they perished. Gus crawled along the floor and peeked out between cracks in the planking as bullets zipped overhead and clanged against the sheet metal roof. Looking out, the field was lit with bright strobes like lightening bugs in the summertime. Tracers arced in and were tearing his men apart. Instead of the open ground and fields of fire being an advantage to the defenders, it was now working against them. Men moved freely in the dark fields to their front, cutting his men down like fish in a barrel. *This isn't like the militias in Ohio and Indiana; this is a trained army.*

Rounds ripped passed him, puncturing through the tower walls. Gus turned his back and dove for the cover of the parapet walkway below as accurate gun fire ripped apart the tower roof and walls. He had to get control of his defense, or he'd lose the compound. Crawling behind the cover of the earthen parapet, he could see that many of his own shooters were hiding the same way. Occasionally, a man would rise up to waste ammunition, firing wildly over the wall at invisible targets.

"Stop shooting, dammit!" he screamed. "Stop shooting at ghosts!"

He continued crawling, steadying his men into cover and readying them for an assault against the walls. The incoming gunfire stopped as the sounds of the infected increased. Gus rose up, daring to take a look. The enemy shooters had vanished. The field to the front now reflected back the gleaming eyes of the infected, drawn in by the gunfire and flares that were still steadily being launched overhead.

"Why aren't the mortars firing back?" Gus yelled at men huddled behind the wall.

"They never come back! We ain't got not mortars," a man hollered back.

The locomotive in the yard roared to life, its whistle blowing as freight car doors were secured. Gus saw fighters in Carson's passenger car with rifles pointed out. Other men were climbing ladders to man small sand bag positions on the roof.

Gus pointed and yelled to one of Carson's

lieutenants in a red beret and tiger striped camouflage directing the loading of the rail cars. "Get those men off the train and on the south wall, we need their help," he shouted.

The lieutenant walked away, ignoring his order. Gus shouted again. This time, the officer turned and looked back at him with contempt. "This isn't our fight. I suggest you get it under control before you find yourself relieved."

The train whistle sounded again, the high pitched shrill barely covering the sound of the infected moans. Flares continued to be fired overhead before raining down from the sky. Gus sat back against the parapet. Looking up, he saw the red and yellow beacons hanging from parachutes. *If this continues, every infected for ten miles is going to descend on us, and we won't have enough people defend all the walls.* He took another quick peek, seeing the infected horde pouring in from the trees. "We need to guide the infected here. We can hold them against this wall," he said to his men near the gates.

A man near the vehicle gate stood and looked out at the approaching mass. He readied a fire bomb, preparing to drop it to lure in the infected. With the Molotov cocktail lit, he readied the overhand toss. Before he could release it, a single shot rang out, the sniper's bullet hitting the man in the chest. The fire bomb dropped to the edge of the wall, setting the man and several others on fire. Gus watched in horror as the man fell over the wall to his death and the others danced in flames, screaming, until they were put down by shooters on the ground.

When Gus went to look again, a sniper's round hit the top of the wall, just missing his head. He ducked back into cover. The infected hit the gate, the momentum of their charge causing it to bow in. "Burn them, but stay in cover!" Gus shouted.

A defender lit another cocktail and let it sail over the wall away from the gate. Others picked up on the move, and more cocktails sailed away, luring the infected away from the gates. Thick, black and grey smoke boiled into the sky. Gus rose up cautiously under the cover of the smoke and looked down at hundreds of gnarled faces screaming back at him.

"Kill them. Kill them all," he said, his men

all standing and raining fire down into the mob below.

Chapter 22

Free Virginia Territories

Brad stood in the shadows, watching the scene play out. He, like most of the others, were now dressed in clean uniforms borrowed from Monty's supplies. He wore an electronic headset, and his chest rig was loaded with full magazines. They'd rested and eaten, trying to prepare for their next move against Crabtree. Just before dark, they had heard the distant train whistle. Hassan had moved out to scout and reported back that a passenger train had entered Crabtree and there were bright lights on inside the walls. Time was running out, and Sean was growing desperate for a plan. Henry claimed to know the prisoner and said he could make him talk.

The prisoner was bound and gagged. Tied to a post in the back of Monty's garage. Henry sat in a chair to Clyde's front, visible under the only light source. The team was gathered around inside but stayed back, hidden in the shadows. The prisoner knew they were there, but he couldn't see their faces. Brad had no misconceptions about torture, and he wasn't even sure if that's what this was. Most of the team was in the dark over the old man's plan, or what he intended to do.

Only two men remained in the main house, held back to monitor the cameras and care for the horses. The old man was holding the curved-blade knife he'd removed from Monty's hand. The handle was black and white, the blade polished steel with jagged teeth, and the entire thing formed into a karambit. Henry carved away at a piece of wood, looking into the wide eyes of the bound man. Henry knew that the man had information, and they needed something to act on.

Brooks walked behind the prisoner and loosened the man's gag. He dropped his hands to Clyde's shoulders and squeezed them, then leaned down and whispered into his ear, "Cooperate, and this will be a lot easier for you." He then walked away, joining the others in the shadows of the room.

Clyde's head swiveled left and right before he focused on Henry, who'd yet to speak. "What the hell do you want from me?" Clyde asked.

Henry continued to whittle at the wood, ignoring his outburst. Taking slow, methodical strokes, he demonstrated the sharpness of the blade. Clyde's head remained still as his eyes shifted, searching the room. The veins on his thick neck had become swollen. Henry stopped his whittling and dropped the scrap of wood at Clyde's feet. "Do you know what this is?" Henry asked, displaying the karambit, twirling it in his hands.

Clyde's lower lip began to tremble. "I'm not the one you want."

"I asked if you knew what this is. I think it's important that you know," Henry repeated.

"I told him we couldn't trust you. We should have shot you dead the day you arrived."

"Answer the damn question," Henry shouted, his voice suddenly hard.

"No, I don't know what the hell it is."

"I didn't think you would." The old man nodded and leaned forward. He let the razor sharp blade nip at the stubble on the man's chin. Clyde froze, holding perfectly still, the blade scraping until Henry pulled away. "This belonged to a friend of mine. It was custom made for him. He carried it everywhere."

Clyde didn't speak; his neck muscles pulsed.

"Do you know where I found this?" Henry asked.

Clyde shook his head.

"I found it in my friend's dead hand. He died right through that door there. Do you know why?"

"Are you going to kill me?" Clyde asked.

"I asked, do you know why?"

"I'm not the one you want. I didn't send the people out here who did this."

"Don't toy with me. I know all about Gus and your bounties. I know he would have asked you to send a team. I want to know the rest. I want to know where the women and children are, I want to know how many, and I want to know when they are leaving."

"You won't kill me; you're the good guys." Clyde said.

Henry locked his eyes on the man across from him. He slowly shook his head. "Oh no, we're not the good guys." Henry looked down at the knife. "And I'm most definitely going to kill you; that decision has already been made. But the thing is, you'll get to decide how fast you die."

Clyde froze in his seat, his back stiff and his jaw quivering. He began blubbering, and mumbling his words. Henry leaned in again and let the blade poke in and slice at the flesh above the man's eye. "Tell me about the train," Henry demanded through gritted teeth.

Clyde shook his head and clenched his eyes shut, trying to blink away a steady stream of blood. "Carson is on the train. He'll bring more men and supplies, then leave with the survivors. They'll pay for me... I have value to them."

"How many survivors?" Henry asked.

"Gus knows me. I can help you; just let me try."

Henry reached forward and nicked a gash above the prisoner's other eye. Clyde shook his head, his voice screeching.

"How many survivors?" Henry asked again.

"More than fifty, less than a hundred," the man said, sobbing.

"How much time we got?"

Clyde let his head hang limp as he spoke just above a whisper. "He doesn't ever stay more than a day... he'll leave tonight or tomorrow morning."

Burt stepped into the light. "What about the men he leaves behind?" he asked.

Clyde looked up and blinked away blood, focusing on the Ranger before turning back to Henry. "They'll leave some men to hold Crabtree, then Gus and the others will continue to follow the tracks south until they establish a new outpost."

Henry pointed the knife at Clyde, the man breaking eye contact and looking away. "And it's at that point where you will seek out and kill survivors, and take away their families?"

The garage door swung open. Cole stood in the doorway, the sounds of automatic weapons fire spilling in behind him. "Something's happening at Crabtree," Cole said.

Henry twirled the blade and pointed it at Clyde. The man shook his head furiously. "I don't know... maybe it's the infected. They bunch up against the gates from time to time."

Sean shrugged his shoulders. "Yeah, could be Primals; maybe they followed the train in."

Cole shook his head. "I don't think so, Chief. From the high ridge, I spotted flares over Crabtree. White and Red."

Sean looked to the others and shot a bright smile. "Sounds like Colonel Cloud and those Rangers have finally shown up. Cole, I want you to take Hassan and try to link up with whoever is hitting Crabtree. Tell them our people are on the train," he said. "Yeah, take Burt with you too."

Burt rose and stepped into the light. "Why me?"

"Because you're the reason we're out here. Now, go and explain to Cloud that things have changed; tell them everything we know."

"And what about you?" Burt asked, holding back.

Sean turned looking at the man in the chair. "We have work to do, same as you. Now, go."

Burt nodded his understanding and quickly moved outside to join the others. Sean passed back to the chair and looked Clyde in the eye. "He's out of time, Henry." Sean looked to the others. "Gather your gear and meet me outside."

Clyde shook violently against his restraints. "But wait—I can tell you more."

"You've violated the law, and we can't let

that stand."

Clyde's jaw dropped open. "Law? There is no law here."

"There's always law. Even without books and courthouses, there is a basic understanding, a moral obligation. You've violated that promise between men. And I'm sorry but justice must be swift." Sean turned away. "A society that fails to deliver justice, fails to survive." He moved outside, the others following close behind, leaving only Henry alone with the man.

Chapter 23

Crabtree, West Virginia
Free Virginia Territories

A relative calm swept over the camp with the soft glow of a pre-dawn horizon. The enemy shooters were gone; the infected lay dead on the ground. His men returned to the watch tower. Binoculars in hand, they searched in all directions. Gus climbed to the top of the parapet and stood next to Bones. He looked down and watched as the last of the women were forced aboard the train. His men were tired and weary, beaten down from losses and the hours long attack. Even with the silence, he couldn't relax; he still had the feeling that they were under siege.

"I think the worst has passed," Bones said. "Must'a been just a bunch of locals trying to start shit before the train leaves."

"No." Gus looked out at the dead infected

on the ground and shook his head. "This isn't over, and the fact that Carson is holding back his troops, I don't think he believes it's over either," he said. "We're in a lot of trouble, Bones. I can feel it." He turned and pointed to the rail cars loaded with the men that were intended as reinforcements to the camp. "Those troops were meant for our push south, but now Carson's got them all in reserve; like he's going to be needing them for his own trip home."

Fighters on top of the cars lay down in firing positions, hidden behind makeshift fortifications on the roof. Gus turned back to the front, trying to interpret the direness of his situation. He placed his hands on the wall and looked out into the darkness. A low mist floated over the snow-covered approach. "No, it's not over. They're still out there and setting up... setting up for something big."

Gus dropped back down to his rear and looked at the loaded train, grimacing at the fresh troops unwilling to help in Crabtree's defense. Carson was ready to flee with a large portion of his guard force. He looked along the grounds; Carson was still nowhere in sight.

"Has Carson come back out of the train since the attack?" Gus asked.

Bones scratched at the back of his neck and shook his head. "No, sir, he's held up in his private train car. You know how he is... he won't come out until the fighting's over."

Gus looked at his scarred hands and rubbed them together. "Bones, go down there, talk to his guard, and find out what their plans are. Maybe you can convince some to stick around."

"You got it, boss," the thin man said, turning to a ladder. Gus looked at the train car. He did know how Carson was; not a coward, just smart. And you don't stay alive in an army filled with bad guys by acting stupid. If Carson didn't make the move to leave, one of his guards would kill him and make the decision for him. These men had no more cause than to enrich themselves and fighting a last stand at an Alamo didn't pay the dividends they were used to. Carson would leave him as soon as he had the chance.

The red-bearded man focused on the

walls, his men still in shock and cowering from the earlier beating, others dead at his feet. These weren't soldiers, but they would hold their ground because they knew that they had no place else to go. There was a hierarchy in Carson's Army and the soldiers in the camp fell far below the men being brought in.

Gus shook his head, looking down at the compound and then overlooking the surrounding terrain. The tactics here were all wrong; they were too far from friendly forces. He began to seriously question Carson's motivations for plunging them so deep into the frontier. Maybe he should go down to the train and have a talk with him. It wasn't too late to load the vehicles and organize a withdrawal back to the north. They could follow the tracks back to friendly ground. He should make a move now, while they still had cover. The enemy were still out there; Gus knew they were surrounded and at a disadvantage. In the daylight, they would attack again, and with no smoke or darkness to hide, they'd be cut down.

A roar turned his head back to the train. The locomotive had ended its low idle and was now thundering at full power, slowly easing toward the secured gate. "*No!* What are you doing?" Bones yelled by the closed railroad gate. He scrambled to open it, seeing that the engineer fully intended on ramming through it. Gus watched in horror as the train increased power and speed before a crunch of steel and wood exploded as the train crashed the barrier.

Gus knew exactly what was happening. Carson was intentionally sacrificing Crabtree to allow for his own escape; gambling that the enemy and infected would focus on the breach instead of pursuing the train. No point in protesting the action, there would be no stopping him. He pulled down his black beanie and watched the train roll through the opening in the wall, leaving the wreckage of the gate in its wake.

He exhaled and squeezed the grip of his pistol, angered at being abandoned. He looked to the ground and saw Bones and others scrambling to seal the breach in the wall. A bulldozer lugged forward, belching black smoke as it plowed toward the hole. The enemy, seeing a new opportunity, opened fire. Rounds pinged off the dozer's front blade. Bones screamed, and Gus looked in his direction in time to see the skinny man clutching his throat, blood seeping between his fingers. Bones was coughing and gurgling blood as he stepped back from the dozer, more rounds catching the man in the chest.

"Get covering fire for that dozer," Gus shouted to his men on the parapet. He rose up and pointed to a distant machine gun, its barrel spitting flame. "There! Fire on that gun, take it out," he bellowed, ordering his men back into the fight. He ran up and down the wall instructing the others to only shoot at the muzzle flashes, focusing their fire on the enemy movements. He stared and watched the train rush away, only a small pack of infected emerging from the mist to chase it. The enemy fire seemed to avoid it, possibly knowing their own people were being held on board.

Now out bound fire was slowing the advance against them. With his men organized and their fire directed, they were slowly beating back the opposing force to the front. Just as Gus started to raise hopes that they could hold the wall, there was an explosion to the west that ripped the rear gate off its hinges. As the smoke cleared, Gus watched hundreds of infected packs running through the hole left in the gate. He quickly realized that they weren't gaining any ground; the only reason the fire dropped to the west was because the enemy had shifted to the east.

Gus called out to the men closest to his side and ordered them to follow. He rolled and slid down the berm, the others following close behind. He hit the ground running and moved toward the country store-turned-headquarters. Not stopping, he crashed through the door and turned to the rifle rack on the wall. He pointed to a machine gun and boxes of ammunition, looked into the face of a frightened man, and directed him to retrieve it.

"We've got to keep the infected back. Take two men and hold them off," Gus said, "You can't let the infected pass. Do you understand?"

Without waiting for an answer, Gus moved to the back of the room and retrieved his own rifle and pack. The sounds of gunfire began popping outside as his men fired on the mob. He stepped back to the open door, standing alone and in the dark. At the front gate, the men were again under heavy fire as the attackers shifted their focus.

Another explosion knocked him back, the flames of the blast warming his face. This time the explosion was against the south wall, located behind the tent city where the berm was weakest. The explosion blew away the logs and breached a third hole in the wall. As the smoke cleared, he saw that it wasn't infected that emerged from the smoke this time, but instead, men in tanned hides and range coats, as well as others in camouflage uniforms.

"Texas..." Gus muttered.

They were now under full assault on three sides. Attacks on both flanks and directly to the front. All of his men were engaged, with nothing left in reserve. At the front where he thought he'd finally organized a defense, his men were panicked and running along the parapet. Looking to the railroad gate, he could see infected moving around the dozer blade. The parapet defenders were pinned down by enemy fire, and the men on the walls couldn't focus on the infected. To the west, even with the help of the machine gun, his men were being overwhelmed as they took fire from the southern breach.

Everything left was pinned by the Texas Rangers moving in from the south. Gus could hear screams of the defenders outside, the ones he'd armed with the machine gun. His arms and legs were shaking with adrenalin; he wanted to be gone, not knowing how everything had changed so quickly. Just a day earlier, he had been sitting comfortably with his men. Now, everything he'd worked for was vanishing all around him. He gritted his teeth and turned back into the store. They wouldn't be able to hold it; it was time for him to retreat. He returned to his corner of the building and retrieved his bug out bag.

For a brief moment, he considered ordering the men to withdraw. The firing outside was frenzied, muzzle flashes and explosions strobing light through the windows of the country store. There was so much automatic weapons fire that he could have sworn they were facing a thousand men. Gus moved to a back wall and opened a door leading into an empty storage area, and then passed by old racks to a window facing the northern wall.

He couldn't save them; if he tried, he would die here. He would let the battle in the compound cover his escape—there was no other way. He looked out into the darkness; the path ahead was still in the shadow of the mountain. All the time he'd spent with these men, Gus intentionally kept himself free of obligations, avoiding friendships or relationships because he knew this day would come. Never did a day pass where he didn't think of this moment; a time when he would have to drop everything to slip away to start over again. Flashes from the fight to the rear lighting his way, he knew the north wall had only seen light engagement. It would be his way out.

Chapter 24

Crabtree, West Virginia
Free Virginia Territories

Brad waited in the dark. His pack loaded and his rifle close to his chest, he sat watching the flashes in the western sky over Crabtree. Joey was standing near the garage door, repeatedly sticking a tomahawk into a tree stump. Henry remained inside, alone with the prisoner. They could hear the fighting at Crabtree, and saw the pops of distant flares floating like stars, twinkling high in the sky to the west. Sean had the saddles off the horses and was rubbing them down with a stiff brush as Shane dropped blankets over their backs.

There was an uncomfortable silence between the men as they waited for Henry to emerge from the garage. Everyone knew what was happening and what needed to be done, but there was no conversation about it. There were side effects from war, and Brad knew that the numbing to violence was one of the biggest. He also knew it was one reason that he and the others took on these tasks — not because they enjoyed them, but because they wanted to spare the others from it. Now he wondered if they'd been wrong to try to stake a home in the wilderness; maybe they should have moved everyone south when they'd had the chance.

Brooks walked from around the back of the house, breaking his thoughts. He stomped his boots on the flagstone path to knock the snow from the treads. The husky, bearded man had his long rifle strapped to his rucksack, and in his arms he cradled a suppressed MP5. "We got a plan, boss?" he asked, looking to Sean.

The chief took a saddle and lay it over the horse's back. Working the straps, he said, "You hear that?" He pointed in the direction of the distant battle. "There has to be at least a battalion fighting it out by the sounds of it."

"That's more than what Cloud could muster," Joey said from the shadows, pulling his hawk from the stump and stepping closer.

Sean nodded and squinted, his eyes studying the distant flares on the horizon. "It has to be the Rangers. Texas must have come through."

Their heads all turned as the garage door opened and Henry stepped out. In his right hand was the bloody karambit. He knelt down and cleaned it in the snow. Raising his head and still kneeling, he peered up at Sean. "You're not going to Crabtree," he said flatly. "You plan to go after the train, don't ya?"

Sean grimaced and dipped his chin. He looked at the men around him and nodded. "We're light fighters; we make our money facing the enemy where he doesn't want us. That compound out there? Crabtree? They picked that spot; adding four or five more men to that fray won't make a difference." Sean sighed and rolled his shoulders. "I pick the train. By the time they clear that open ground, they'll think they made an escape, they'll let their guard down, and that's when we'll get our turn."

"You can't blow the tracks with your people on board."

Sean rubbed his eyes and bit at his lip. "We'll have to find a way on the train."

"I thought you might say that. There's a place close to here... a set of narrow turns where the train enters the mountain. You can catch it there."

Sean nodded. "Lead the way then. I've heard the train whistle, and I don't think we have much time if we want to catch it."

Henry shook his head. "I'm not going with you. I have a score of my own to settle back at Crabtree."

Shane stopped what he was doing with the horse and stepped close to the old man. "You're going after Gus?" he asked. "You don't have to do that; you can go home."

Henry nodded and sheathed the karambit. "This has to stop here." The old man's jaw tensed. He reached into his pocket and removed the pipe as he looked up at Sean. "You make sure it's done. Carson doesn't leave that train."

"We'll make sure of it," Sean said.

Shane stepped closer and pulled his pack to his shoulders. "I'm going with you."

Henry shook his head no and turned away. He tamped the tobacco and placed the unlit pipe in the crease of his mouth. "Your little girl will be on the train, so you need to make sure she's safe. What needs doing, I can do on my own." He moved to the horses and removed a saddle bag from a fence post, transferring items into an olive green pack. "Take the horses back the way we came. When you get to the train tracks, go right. You'll find a series of sharp bends. At the second bend, the train will slow enough that you can board. It's a blind corner, they won't be able to see you."

"Where do we leave the horses?" Sean asked.

Henry grinned, running a hand over the neck of the large line back, the horse moving toward his touch. "Don't worry about these girls; they know their way home," he whispered. The old man slung his rifle and turned toward the distant flares. "It won't be long now; you should get on your way." Without saying anything more, he turned and walked away, fading into the darkness.

Wind blew through the tall trees, the distant fighting mixing with the cracking of the limbs. With Brooks and Sean in the front, Brad joined the others and mounted the trail horse, Joey and Shane riding double to the rear. As Brooks led the way, Brad's horse fell in and followed along without command. Riding on, he let his mind wander, wondering about where they were going and what they would do when they got there. He looked at his gloved hands and the fresh uniform. He was a soldier again. No matter how often he thought he'd left it all behind, somehow it called him back. He hung his head, comfortable in the saddle, and let the horse take him.

With the blowing of the train's whistle getting closer, the horses turned onto a narrow trail and skillfully descended the terrain until finding the railroad bed. Brooks guided them right and along a packed, earthen trail. The railroad tracks sloped in a lazy arc against the cut sides of the mountain, curving slowly to the right then making a sharp S-turn around the face of a top ridge. Brooks pulled up and dismounted, then removed his gear from the horse and stepped away. After the other men had done the same and were all on the ground, Shane shooed the horses away from the tracks and up the trail that led up the ridge; soon they were out of sight.

Brooks walked along the tracks and up onto a tall, rock overhang. "Looks like a good place to drop on."

Sean grimaced and looked up and down the tracks, then dipped his chin. "The train will have to slow down here. The old man was right; this is the perfect spot. Okay, move us up."

Brad moved to the side of the ledge and watched as the others climbed the surface of the rock, then he followed Joey to the top. On the overhang, they could see the glow of the train's light and hear the rumble of its engines. Sean and Brooks moved out to the rock face and readied their scoped rifles. "Brooks and I will drop any shooters; you three need to drop on to the train. We'll be right behind you. Power on your headsets; they're low on power, but they should work at close range."

Joey slung his rifle across his back. He pushed a green cup against his ear, then adjusted the foam microphone so that it was just over the corner of his mouth. Joey drew his side arm and tactical tomahawk and squatted at the ledge, looking down. *"That's a long way down, boss,"* he said over the radio, the voice coming back metallic.

Sean smiled. *"It isn't the fall I'm worried about,"* he said before his face turned cold. *"Listen, we don't know what we're getting into down there, so be dynamic, move fast, and kill anything trying to kill you. Wherever you land, fight your way to the front of the train and clear the cars as you move."*

Brad drew back the bolt of his rifle and verified the chamber with the glint of brass. He crept into position behind Joey and tapped him on the shoulder to let the man know he was there. "We got this, Bro," he heard Joey whisper.

"We got this," Brad answered back.

"There it is," Shane called from the front as the train's light intensified from the blind corner. The locomotive came around the corner, its big diesel engine leading the way, moving slow but closing fast. It had a total of six sections: an engine on both ends, three box cars, and a passenger car at the front.

Brad saw the flash of the SEALs' rifles as they opened fire on the train, knocking men off the top with precise aim. Men dropped from the tops of the cars while tracers raced up at them as guards fired back. Shane stepped forward and looked back at them with false bravado. "Just like jump school," he shouted before stepping off and dropping out of sight.

"Get some," Joey screamed, launching himself into the air. Brad looked down to see the man land on the back end of the first box car in a perfect parachute landing fall, rising up with the hawk swinging. With no time to be scared, Brad sprung forward and felt the momentary freefall before landing hard on the roof of the second car, enveloped in darkness, he shook the rattle from his knees. Muzzle flashes of guards firing at him lit his way as he rolled to the side and pumped the trigger, rounds tearing into the men at his front. Sean and Brooks fired down and disappeared from Brad's sight when the train moved around a bend. Using the train's sharp turn to his advantage, Brad got to his feet and dashed forward, the swaying train making it difficult to stay on his feet.

He dropped to a sandbag barrier, taking fire from another set of guards ahead of him. Heavy rounds from AK-47s filled the air with automatic weapons fire from the front and back. Brad's ears, covered with the headset, were muffled from the zipping and buzzing of near misses, noise as ferocious as a burning hornet's nest. The sandbags burst, spitting sand and dirt into his face. Brad rolled out away from the barrier and rose with his rifle. Instead of taking cover, the guards ahead were kneeling in the open. Brad fired, hitting one, stitching the man across his chest.

He shifted his point of aim to the second guard. Pulling the trigger, he watched as the man spun left and fell from the train. He heard Shane shouting as he moved up beside him and dove into the bags.

"Everyone make it?" Sean asked over the radio.

"I'm here," Brad checked in, keeping his head down.

"Joey is covering our rear. He won't let anything from the front get to us. We're holding the first and second box cars," Shane said, turning to his side to reload his rifle. *"They're dug in good on the passenger car to the front."*

"Keep the pressure on," Sean said, his radio clicking dead. *"Take your car and move forward."*

Brad rose back up, looking to the distant cars at the back. The train left the tight bend and began to straighten. Entering a downward slope, the early morning sun broke the mountain and began to shine on them. He could see the SEALs engaged in a firefight with men in tiger-striped uniforms near the rear locomotive.

"They're on the engine," Brad said, ducking back into cover as more guards climbed a ladder and opened up on them. Brad pulled back behind the sand bags. As he moved, his boots scraped a hinge and he spotted a locked hatch at his feet. He pointed at it. "We need to get down there," he said, raising up to fire on the approaching guards.

"They'll have hostages," Shane said. "We open this hatch and we'll be right in the line of fire."

Brad grimaced, knowing he was right. "One of us will have to go down while the other pops the hatch."

Shane released another burst of gunfire then looked back at Brad. "There won't be any sneaking."

Brad pushed forward to his elbows and fired multiple three round bursts at the guards to his front. Another hit, the target falling to the decks as another fled back off the train car. "Give me a thirty count and pop that lock!" he said, scrambling to his feet and rushing to the end of the car. Brad leapt the sandbag barriers. "Shit," he yelled, barely keeping his balance. He lost his footing on the slick roof and, moving like an out of control ball player, he dropped and slid the last few feet before catching the edge of the car and the ladder. Hooking a gloved hand on the top rung, he swung off the back side of the boxcar.

Dangling over the edge, he saw a man

look up at him with bug eyes; the tiger-striped guard struggled to raise his rifle. Not hesitating, Brad swung outward and kicked the man in the face. Brad fell with the man, the both of them landing on a narrow platform below, lying side by side. The bug eyes rose first, struggling for a holstered side arm. Brad lunged at him, using his left hand to press the man's weapon into the chest holster.

Brad rolled the man, pinning him against the wall. With the distance closed and his left hand still on the holstered pistol, Brad grasped the knife on his vest. In one smooth motion, he drew the knife and drove it deep between the guard's ribs. The guard shuddered and dropped his pistol hand, then flailed and grabbed at Brad's knife arm. With the knife still stuck between the man's ribs, Brad rose up and rained down a stiff blow to the man's jaw. The guard's grip relaxed, but he was still alive, foam and blood spitting from his mouth. Brad tucked his hands, grabbed the man by his collar, and rolled him over and off the car's small platform.

As the guard screamed while falling to the tracks, Brad heard the gunshots of Shane blowing the lock.

"Hatch is open. I'm taking fire."

He knew he had to move or Shane would be cut in half. Brad scrambled back to his feet and pressed against a small steel door cut into the side of the car. No time to estimate his rounds, he let the partially filled magazine drop to the deck as he loaded a fresh one. A woman's screams pierced the air from the far side of the door. No more time to wait, he grasped the handle and pushed, rolling into the opening.

He flew in, crashing into the back of a guard that was looking at the hatch near the center of the car. The boxcar was jammed full of people. Distracted by the open hatch, neither of the guards turned around to see him enter. Two guards standing watch at each end had their rifles up and were aiming at the hatch. Brad pressed the muzzle of his M4 between the nearest guard's shoulder blades and pulled the trigger. The gunshot boomed in the enclosed space and the man fell forward, shocking the guard beside him. Brad spun in the close quarters and caught the next guard just below the jaw with the stock of his rifle. The guard's neck cracked, his head flying back.

The women in the car, seeing what was happening, pressed away from the fight. Moving in a thick pack, they lunged and overwhelmed the remaining guards, pressing them against the far wall of the car.

"I'm in!" Brad yelled into the mic. *"Clear."*

Brad looked back to the front and watched Shane drop through the hatch and into the group of women, who now had the guard's rifles. The disarmed men's heads were pressed against the front wall of the car with the muzzles against the backs of their necks. Brad pushed his way through, guiding the women behind him. With the women clearing a path, the two soldiers took control of the guards and ordered the armed women to cover the rear.

"Second car is clear," Brad said over the radio. The sounds of gunfire still echoed from the front of the train.

"Third car is clear," they heard Brooks respond. *"How you doing up front, Joey?"*

"I'm lying on the first car; hatch is open. They

got some people inside, but only a couple shooters. I got this passenger car to my front pinned but not for long, I could use some help, fellas," Joey answered.

"We're coming to you on the high road," Sean said.

He clenched his fist. Brad looked across at Shane and saw him nod his head. *"We'll take the low road,"* Brad called out.

The prisoners stood with their arms up at the front end of the boxcar at either side of another door cut into the end. This door, unlike the last, was held shut with a large bolt. Brad let his rifle hang from the sling and drew his pistol. He shoved the prisoner nearest him back and spun the man to face the wall, then pressed his face against it.

Tunnel vision now closing in on the single hatch to his front, he moved in and pressed the pistol's barrel against the prisoner's temple. Brad's left hand grabbing a fist full of fabric from the back of the man's shirt, he pulled him away from the wall. Shane pulled the second prisoner away from the wall and shoved him at the door. Turning back, he told the women to take cover by the sides of the car. "Open the door," Brad said, looking at the second guard.

The prisoner's shaky hand grabbed at the bolt lock and drew it back. Before the hatch could fully open, automatic gunfire sparked along the door frame. With the second prisoner cut down, Brad rushed forward, using the other as a shield. The door blew in, revealing a shooter firing a small rifle from the hip. Brad extended his arm and fired as he ran the man ahead, feeling the man shudder as rounds impacted with his body. Shoving the dead shield forward, Brad fired at the men across from him until his weapon was empty. From above, he saw the SEALs leap over his head to the first boxcar.

"Dropping into car one," Brooks yelled over the radio.

Brad, outside and alone now, stepped away from the door. Shane quickly moved out onto the boxcar deck beside him and assessed the opening of the first car. Flashes of light coming from inside let them know someone was in there. Brad felt a burning at his face and touched a gash on his check where a round had creased his skin. He sucked in dirty air and jumped to the next car, hitting the entrance in a sprint.

The small space was lit only by a swinging lamp. He stood solemnly, his mind clouded, searching the confused gazes of the survivors lining the walls of the boxcar. Brad could still hear Joey's rifle above pinning the men on the passenger car. The interior of first boxcar was filled with smoke. Sean and Brooks were in the center, standing over dead guards. Brad stepped forward and saw a hostage's body at his feet. "Oh my god," he said with a gasp and flinching back.

Looking down at the wood decking, he saw bodies covered the floor—civilian bodies. Sean dropped his head. "They started shooting, killing them, and we had to go in blind."

Brad turned and watched Shane step into the boxcar. The young soldier peered into the dark, his gaze surveying the dimly lit space. A girl emerged from the shapeless figures against the wall; she ran and leapt into his arms. Shane lifted her to his chest and held her tight. "Ella, thank god. Are you okay?" he asked. The girl didn't respond, burying her face against his shoulder.

Joey looked into the open hatch. "They just put something between the cars. I think they're going to try and blow the coupler."

Sean nodded looked behind him at the bolted door leading forward. "Get everyone to the back of the train. We need to get out of here. We'll hunt Carson after we get these people to safety."

"No," Ella shouted. "Chelsea is in the front!"

Chapter 25

Crabtree, West Virginia
Free Virginia Territories

Rapid gunfire from behind and drawing closer solidified his reasoning to flee. Crabtree was overrun. Gus pulled through the window and dropped into the high drifted snow behind the store building. A staccato of rifle shots urged him to duck his head and get low. He crawled forward, pulling himself into the tall grass. Moans of the infected and the screams of his men increased his fear. He hugged the ground and crawled forward. Men with rifles let loose long bursts of automatic weapons fire. The chatter of M4s mingled with the howls of the infected and the screams of victims.

Tracers arced over his head, forcing it down. Men were firing at anything that moved. They were in a panic and looking for a way out. Gus peeked above the grass. He saw two fighters approaching him. Too dark and impossible to tell friend from foe, he shouldered his rifle and fired at them. The first man was hit with a three-round burst to the chest. The second dropped his rifle in an attempt to surrender. Gus rose to his feet and fired again, knocking the surrendering man to the ground. More rounds raced in at him as someone opened up with a machine gun. He dove back to the ground and crawled away, under the reach of the gunfire.

When the machine gun shifted fire away from him and toward other targets, Gus dashed forward. He raced to the safety of the wall before hearing a noise behind him. He thought he heard trucks before more automatic weapons fire flashed from the direction of the main gate. Rounds slapped and ricocheted off the store building now far behind him.

He froze, hearing the swishing of grass, a steady drum beat of footfalls, and the gurgled growl of the infected. He spun back, tucking his rifle as he moved. Trying to focus in the darkness, he peered ahead and saw the silhouettes of four infected men running directly at him. He fired two hasty shots, then ducked low as the first leapt, tossing it over his back. Squaring up back to the front, he gut shot the next one, then deflected another with a hard bash from a thrown shoulder. Two more attackers cut in from his flank. They bore down on him and he raised rifle again, only to find the bolt locked back on an empty chamber. Gus flinched back, anticipating the creatures' bite.

Two loud gunshots rang out from his blind spot. The attacking Primals crashed to the ground, one taking out Gus's legs and knocking him to the field as it fell. A sturdy man stepped over him, reached down, and pulled him to his feet. Gus used a sleeve to wipe his face of blood and gore. He looked up into the face of the old bounty hunter.

"Henry, thank god you're here. Where are the others?" he said.

"Waiting for us. I came back to get you," the old man said, still holding his lever action rifle and looking off at the fighting within the compound. Infected attackers were back lit by the fires of the burning camp. "You going somewhere?"

Gus nodded eagerly. "Yeah, getting the hell out of here." Adjusting his grip on the rifle, he searched his kit for another magazine. Not finding one, he looked up at Henry and said, "You have any more ammo?"

The old man grinned and shook his head as he nodded to the lever action rifle. "Nothing for that."

"Dammit," Gus grunted, tossing the empty M4 into the grass. He turned and stepped toward the wall. "Where'd you say the boys were?"

Henry stood his ground, still facing the fight in the compound. "You're going to leave 'em?"

"That's exactly what I intend to do." Gus moved on, leaving the old man to follow along behind him. He stepped heavily through the tall wet grass, the fires from the compound lighting his way. He debated in his mind what he would do when they reached the wall. They would be okay; they had the horses, and five men would do fine out here. He could follow the tracks back north, regroup with Carson, and start over. *But what if Carson turns me away?* That was a possibility after his failure there. Screw it then, he'd skip Carson and set off on his own to rebuild. There was plenty of land and opportunities to the west.

Chris and Clyde knew his value and would follow him anywhere. The two new men were experienced and, with his leadership, they could go anywhere. He approached the wall and walked along the tall, earth embankment, searching for a ladder that would bring him to the top. He turned back and looked at Henry, who was following some distance behind. He watched as the intensity of the gunfire diminished; it would take him some time to build another army of this size. None of that mattered though; this wasn't about victories for him, it was about survival. Henry drew close and stopped just feet away, cradling the rifle in his arms.

"Where did you cross the wall?" he asked, looking over his shoulder.

Henry pointed with the barrel of his rifle. "Just ahead there at the low point."

"Why didn't the cousins come across with you?"

Henry let out a long breath and slung the rifle over his shoulder. From his pocket, he fished out his pipe and began filling it with tobacco. "I wonder how many families are without a husband or a father because of what you've done here."

Gus stopped and turned to face him. "Don't go getting sentimental on me, old man. Where the hell are the cousins?"

Henry cupped his hand around the pipe, shielding the light from his match as he lit it. He puffed in and exhaled the gray smoke. "It's already too late for that I'm afraid."

"What the hell is that supposed to mean?"

"Sentimentality, that is. I didn't come here to help you escape."

Gus smiled and took a threatening step forward, squaring his broad shoulders toward the old man. "So, what? You going to kill me?" Gus said. "For what? Leaving these animals behind? For trying to clean up this country?"

Henry smiled, not intimidated. He drew in another breath of the tobacco then exhaled, blowing the smoke into Gus's face. "No, I'm going to kill you for sending killers to my home."

"You're talking in riddles, old man. Now let's get out of here before I flatten you."

Henry let the pipe rest between his teeth. "The kid I mentioned — Ricky? I never met him on the road, never talked to him about you having work, never talked to him about bounties. Nope, I met Ricky when he and a couple of your boys went to the west slope, just like you told them to. Yeah, and they found my place. They found me."

"And what? You killed them?"

"I did," Henry said. "But not until Ricky told me all about you."

"Why, you..." Gus stepped inside and swung up his right arm, but Henry anticipated the attack. His karambit un-sheathed, he ducked under Gus's arm and slashed upward, the curved blade cutting deep into the big man's flank. Henry yanked back, withdrawing the knife and slashing opening Gus's side. The big man tried to grab him, but Henry was just as strong and flung the man back and down into the grass.

Gus twisted in agony and put a hand to his side, pulling back fingers coated in hot, sticky blood. He dug his heels into the ground and tried to push away from the old man standing over him with the now glistening blade. He coughed in pain, clenching his teeth. The old man looked down at him and shook his head. "The infected will come for you now," he said just above a whisper. "Do you smell it? The coppery tang of your own blood?"

"Screw you," Guns said. Pushing away with his heels and rolling to his belly, he crawled to the wall.

Henry walked and stood over him. "Why bother running? Even in death you're a coward, Gus; even cut wide open and bleeding out, you won't turn back to face what haunts you."

Gus rolled to his back and clenched his fists. "Then just kill me."

The old man shook his head in disgust,

looking at the gaping wound in the man's gut. He took the pipe from his mouth and knocked the spent ashes onto Gus's quivering legs. Placing the pipe back into his shirt pocket, he turned and walked away. Looking over his shoulder, he said, "You're already dead."

Chapter 26

Free Virginia Territories

"What?" Brad said, turning to face Ella.

"She's up there," Ella gasped. "The man took her... they made Chelsea go to the front."

"No!" Brad yelled, looking back to the head of the car. Sean and Brooks were pushing the survivors past him to the rear of the train. "I have to go," he said, turning to run to the front. He collided with the bolted door, then flung back the lock and let the door swing open. He found the platform deserted. Looking down at the coupler holding the cars together, he saw a small gray lump pressed against the mechanism and a long string of time fuse belching black smoke. He bent his knees and leapt the gap to the opposing platform, fractions of a second before the blast threw him against the wall and rattled the car.

The coupler broke free, releasing the back of the train. He lay on the platform of Carson's passenger car watching the rest of the train fade out of sight. Fighters looked down at him from the roof, and he scrambled to avoid their gunshots that pinged off the deck. He'd dropped his rifle and now only had the suppressed M9 pistol to return fire. He huddled low and pressed against the steel walls of the platform. Behind, he watched Brooks and Sean stepping onto the fading boxcar's deck. They fired precision shots into the men on the train's roof as the separation increased. *"We'll find you,"* Sean said over the static filled radio. *"Stay alive and we'll find you."*

Brad watched as his friends faded from sight. He shook his head and took off the headset, tossing it to the tracks speeding past below. With the enemies above him dead, the sounds of gunfire stopped. He moved to a squat and pressed his back against the bulkhead behind him. He listened intently, the noise from the diesel electric engine and the clacking of the tracks filling the air. He shimmied to the right of the door and cautiously stood up. This door, unlike the others, slid in and was slightly ajar.

Brad switched the pistol to his left hand and cautiously slid the door completely open.

Edging around the corner, he looked down a long, narrow corridor with several evenly spaced doors on the left and right side of the passage. He stepped inside, letting the door slide shut behind him and silencing much of the noise. On the floor five feet to his front was a man gasping for air, a foaming gunshot wound at the center of his chest. Brad stepped into the passageway and stood over the man before pumping two suppressed rounds in the man's skull. With a last gasp, the man's head dropped to the floor.

Ahead in the long, narrow hallway, the lights flashed and flickered. He stopped and listened for noise from the compartments; he had no idea how many of Carson's men remained. Brad stiffened and bent his elbows, letting the suppressed pistol lead the way. Slowly he crept forward, the clicking of the road wheels on the tracks filling the passageway. The light flickered overhead; he fired shots into the clear plastic cover, killing the distracting flicker and enclosing the car in darkness. The only light that remained came from under the doors leading to the private cabins.

He stopped at the first door on the left, hiding his head from the window. He pushed it in and moved around the corner, following his gun's muzzle into the space. Seeing it was a private cabin filled with canned goods and boxes, he pulled back and spun into the hallway, repeating the same procedure in the cabin to his right. Moving back to the hallway, he stepped to the next door and again opened it and swept inside.

He heard a cracking of broken glass behind him and dove to the cabin's floor. The window above his head exploded, furious cold air rushing into the confined space. Brad stretched to the side, extended the pistol into the void behind him, and began rapidly pulling the trigger, firing blind. As the last brass cartridge expelled from his pistol, the gunfire stopped. He rolled to his back, dropped the magazine, and racked the slide. He edged forward and looked into the dead eyes of a man holding a submachine gun. A red beret tipped from the side of the dead man's head; expanding red stains blotched the chest of his tiger-striped camouflage. Stretching into the passageway, he snatched away the UMP .45-caliber submachine gun and removed spare magazines from the guard's body, then ducked back into cover.

Reloading both weapons, he sat listening and waiting for another attack. He slid to the compartment door and peeked into the passageway, finding nothing but darkness. Quietly, he rose back to his feet and pivoted into the hall. He holstered the M9 and led the way with the muzzle of the UMP 45, swinging into the next cabin. Bringing up the muzzle, he found himself looking at a restrained woman, hands and feet tied and an orange sack over her head. Behind her was a large man. He had the woman's head locked in a tight grip and a pistol to her temple.

Brad raised the submachine gun and aimed at the man's face. "So, you must be Carson. I didn't expect to find you hiding behind a woman."

The big man shook his head. "No, no, no. That's not what this is; I'm offering to make you a deal. You wouldn't have come up here if she wasn't important to you."

Brad forced a laugh. "What's important to me is that you die."

"Die? Die for what? What would that solve?"

Brad looked at him, his jaw quivering, not knowing how to respond.

Carson pressed the barrel closer to Chelsea's head and smiled at Brad. "I'm just doing what others have been afraid to do. I'm trying to start something new again. I'm bringing us back. Hiding behind walls? Is that what the future of man is? I don't think so."

"You killed my people," he said.

"Killed people? I'm *saving* people, and bringing everyone back. People have a future with me."

Brad shook his head, "Doesn't matter. I came here to stop you."

"For who? Texas? You want to give them all the power?"

Brad exhaled and blinked his eyes. He kept the sights on Carson's head as he rolled his neck. "I'm tired. If you want to talk about this then let her go, find some beers, and we can chat. Otherwise, I'm going to pump .45 slugs into your brain bucket."

The man shook his head. "Now, back up, soldier boy. We both know that isn't true."

Brad held his position, looking the man in the face. He wanted nothing more than to pull the trigger and watch the rounds tear into the man's forehead. It was the professional in him that prevented it; that and the fear that something would go wrong and Chelsea would be killed.

"I don't think you're half as tough as you're pretending to be. If you were, I'd already be dead." The big man grinned as he released the woman's head just enough to remove the cover, revealing Chelsea's fear-filled eyes. Her jaw trembled. As she looked at Brad, a tear formed and rolled to the corner of her lip.

"Aww, now look at that," Carson said, seeing the expression on the soldier's face change. "Looks like the soldier boy has a soft side after all."

Brad's hand squeezed the pistol grip. "Let her go," he said.

"Uh—no, that's not how this works," Carson spat back. "If you want me to let her go, you'll do exactly as I say."

Brad gripped the submachine gun tight and pulled it into the pocket of his shoulder. If he was going to win this fight, he needed an edge. "Listen up, shithead. I have a gun pointed at your face. Let her go or I'll bust your grape the way I did your son's."

The man's face flushed. "What?" Carson said, the pitch in his voice changing. "What do you know about my son?"

"Does a skinny little punk by the name of Carl ring a bell? Ugly as fuck, carried a chrome shotgun?"

"Impossible."

"He was a real asshole. Dead as shit now, though. I shot him in the face and barbecued his body for the infected to feast on."

Carson mashed his teeth and shoved the woman away, bringing the pistol in Brad's direction. The soldier's finger already taking the slack from the trigger, the submachine gun spit rounds that tore through the man's skull, snapping his head back into the shattered window behind him. Chelsea pulled away and, with a swift front kick, Brad launched the man's body from the broken cabin window.

Chapter 27

He found the engine empty, the engineers either dead or had abandoned the train. Brad stopped the locomotive at a ghost town some hundred miles over the Ohio border. She was sitting in a sleeper car, two loaded packs at her feet, rifles strapped to the top of each. She smiled up at him and handed off a half-eaten can of fruit cocktail.

"Will this stop them?" Chelsea asked.

Brad took the can and stood in the doorway of the sleeper car. He shook his head and stepped toward her. "Someone else will take his place... someone always will."

"And then what?"

Brad shrugged. "Texas can figure that out." He looked down at the backpacks and held his gaze on them. "Are you sure about this?" he said, sitting on a bunk across from her. "I figured out how to stop this thing, I'm sure I could figure out how to take it back."

"Would you stay with me?"

He turned toward her and smiled grimly. "I can't stay there."

"Then I won't go back."

"What about Ella and Shane?" Brad said, breaking eye contact and looking away.

"Shane wasn't happy there either; he's always wanted to take Ella to Texas. Without me holding him back, maybe he'll finally do it."

"They'll worry about you."

"I'll leave a note for them, Shane will understand."

"And Ella?"

"She needs a real home, someplace safe in the south. Shane can give that to her."

Slowly, he shifted his weight from the bunk and rose up, pulling the pack to his shoulders. Chelsea did the same and followed him down the passageway of the train car. They were stopped over a northwest intersection, a blacktop road just on the outskirts of some no name town. Brad jumped to the ground and helped Chelsea down behind him. The air was cold, much colder than it had been back in West Virginia. There was no snow on the ground, and the blacktop was a sun-bleached charcoal. The sun cast a gray light through the heavy cloud cover.

It felt good having his boots back on the ground; he stepped away from the train and used his binoculars to search the terrain ahead. An empty street, vandalized and long ago looted buildings and homes. This was a dead land, dead to everything — including the Primals. He walked slower than usual, keeping to the center of the road with Chelsea just behind him. They passed by homes with broken windows and grass as high as the mailboxes.

They'd stopped to investigate several cars. Beyond repair, gas tanks punctured and drained, upholstery and wiring all cannibalized for other uses. At the edge of the town was a river and a two lane bridge. There had been a fire, the buildings scorched with nothing left but charred frames and ashes. On the far side of the river was a welcome sign and an ancient, defeated roadblock made of burned out police cars. The name of the town on the welcome sign had been painted over in bold red with *Hell, population zero, stay away.*

Brad walked slowly around the barrier, kneeling to lift pieces of spent brass in his cupped hand. He turned to Chelsea, showing them to her as he tossed them to the grass. "5.56 and .40 caliber," he said holding one up. "Police and military." He shook his head and let them fall back to the road where they clanged and rolled away.

"Why haven't we seen any of the infected here?" she asked.

"Because they left, the same as the people. There's no food here and Primals have to eat, the same as us." Brad stood and turned to face the distant trees. "They'll be in there, living off the land like the APEX predators they are now."

The pair continued on. Leaving the town, the terrain became more flat and was surrounded by grasslands. Farmers' fields reclaimed by nature were filled with small saplings and overgrown with weeds. Near the end of the day, Brad spotted a deer but let it go, not wanting to risk a gunshot so close to dark. They walked past a farm. The house's windows and doors were broken, the barn reduced to ashes. Decomposed bodies hung from a tall oak tree in the front yard. They moved quickly past it, not speaking, but holding their rifles close.

A wooden billboard at the intersection of a country road advertised fresh produce. They took the turn, following the sign and staying north. At the top of a hill, they rested and surveyed the small town ahead. Like the one before, this place was mostly burned. Wind blew in Brad's face and drops of icy snow pelted against his cheeks, reminding him to find shelter. He used his binoculars to search the small town. Cold and gray, there were no signs of life; no movement, no flickering lights, no smoke from a welcoming fire. The closest building was a small, white house set just off the road. Behind it was a steel, pole barn and a fenced-in yard filled with rusted tractors.

It was never safe to approach unknown

terrain from the high ground and crossing in the open, so they went to the back of the hill and moved into the tall fields. The going was slower, but it allowed them to circumvent the hill and approach the pole barn unseen. The building was unlocked, a rusty hasp pulled back with a crow bar that still lay on the ground. The door was shut and Brad slid it open just enough so they could pass though.

The inside was dark and cold, the floor filled to shoulder height with tractor and automotive parts. Brad held a flashlight and inspected the space, ready to turn away and check the house when Chelsea pushed him inside and closed the door behind them. "No, this is good; nobody will come here," she whispered.

Brad wended around the piles of scrap, finding a section of bare floor in the back corner near a drill press and workbench constructed of old lumber. They dropped their gear just as the wind outside picked up and sleet began to pelt the steel building. It was very cold, and the wind crept in through every crevice of the pole barn. He found an old paint can and used his tomahawk to break down the wooden bench. Using the scraps, he built a hot fire from the dry bits of wood. Sitting together, wrapped in a wool blanket, Brad drifted off to sleep watching a can of soup boil on the fire.

When he woke, the fire was out. His face was cold, but she was wrapped around him, and under the wool blankets he was warm. The wind rattled the steel sides of the building and he could hear their moans. The Primals were awake and on the hunt. Moving in from the surrounding forest and grasslands, they would search for food. He lay awake until dawn, listening to her breathe, flinching at the howl of every Primal, and trying to estimate their distance and numbers in his head. Silently, he was coordinating a plan if they managed to get inside.

When the first rays of morning shone through holes in the building, he carefully crawled from the blankets. Stirring the coals and adding more fuel, he lit another fire, making a light meal of boiled oats for their breakfast. Chelsea woke and sat up, watching him with the blankets still draped over her shoulders. He stirred the contents and handed her a half share in a plastic bowl.

Taking a bite with a brown plastic spoon, she looked up at him. "Why did you leave the camp?"

"Why stay?" he said, passing her a plastic bear filled with honey.

"You could have stayed for me."

"You knew where I went; you never came or sent word."

Shaking her head, she stuffed her blankets and gear back into her pack. "We should get going; we don't want to waste the light."

They passed through the remains of the burned out town late in the morning. Garbage and weed-covered sidewalks flanked rusted cars on flat tires. Near the center of the town was a barricaded police station. Another last stand for humanity. Draped over coiled wire and sandbags were decomposed, leathered remains. Brad stepped close to one of the bodies and Chelsea grabbed his wrist, trying to pull him back. When he resisted, she let go, allowing him to step near the body.

A police officer lay on his back. The man's face was gone to the skull. He wore a dark blue police jacket with an army green tactical vest over it. His rifle was rusted and frozen into his skeletal grip. Brad stopped and looked the man over, then let his eyes take in the full scene of the carnage. "One day they just made a final stand," he said. "And nobody came for them; nobody came to bury them. Nobody will ever know about this battle; nobody will ever write about it."

"Is this how the world ended?" Chelsea asked.

Brad looked up and felt the wind in his face as it began to snow again. He shook his head and looked away. At the edge of the police building was a line of squad cars and utility vehicles, all on flat tires except an old, diesel tow truck. He stepped closer, then turned back to Chelsea. "Could you get this running?"

She stared at the truck and nodded her head. "If you can get me something to jump the battery, I'm sure I could."

"Well, you're the mechanic. You got any ideas?" Brad asked.

She turned back and pointed at the police station. "Look for a generator. They would have had them out back." Without waiting for his response, she approached the tow truck. Reaching through the open driver's window, she popped the hood.

"Be careful," he said, looking at her.

"I got it. Go find a generator."

Brad looked back to the police building. He walked closer and followed the sidewalk lined with police vehicles to where it met a tall block fence. From the top, he saw a two foot long pipe and strands of barbered wire; following along, he found a rusted cipher lock with eight worn key buttons. Brad grabbed the gate and found it too sturdy to try prying open. He pulled his suppressed pistol and, leaning off to the side, he fired three times, the final shot cutting away the pin holding the cipher lock to the hasp.

"Are you okay?" he heard Chelsea call

from the front.

"I'm fine, just opening a door."

Brad pushed the gate in and saw fresh snow lined the parking lot; not a single foot print had disturbed it. He stepped into the yard and walked between dumpsters and empty pallets with FEMA markings. In the back of the yard was a neatly arranged row of black body bags, covered with just a dusting of snow. He avoided the area and moved closer to the police building. Near a bay door, he found what he was looking for. Beyond a pile of empty fuel drums and gas cans was neat line of red generators. Brad moved along the generators and checked the fuel tanks, finding all of them empty. "Probably ran themselves dry after the attack with nobody left to fill them," he said to himself.

He reached for a small gallon gas can and felt the liquid slosh around inside. Turning back to the generators, he searched them until he found one that had multiple power jacks and jumper cables built into the side. Grabbing both he returned to the front of the station to see Chelsea digging through a tool box in the back of the truck. He set the generator near the front of the truck, opened the gas cap, and prepared to fill it from the can.

"Wait," Chelsea said. She pulled a canvas bag from the tool box and carried it to the street. Digging through the bag she pulled out two bottles of dry gas and a can of starter fluid. Chelsea took the gallon gas can and shook it. "This'll help with the water," she said before filling the generator. "Give me your pack." Brad did as she said. She took their bags and loaded them into the back of the truck, tying them down with bungee straps.

"What about the truck?" Brad said. "You need to treat that too?"

"I hope not. The truck's tank is full and if it's stayed sealed up tight, we might be okay."

"Might? And if not?"

Chelsea shrugged. "Fuel filter should help us out, but after that we keep our fingers crossed." She finished filling the generator, moved it closer to the front end of the tow truck, and made sure the 12 volt cables would reach. She pulled out the hand crank and waved a hand to Brad. He took over, the cord pulling hard, but on the fifth tug the small generator came to life. Chelsea adjusted the idle and quickly had it revving.

"Brad," she said.

He looked up. Her mouth open, he followed Chelsea's gaze to a brick apartment building across the street. On the second floor, faces looked out at them. Cold gray faces with gnarled teeth, hands clenched in boney fists. "Start the truck!"

Chelsea stretched the cables to the truck's battery and entered the cab. Brad moved beyond it and readied himself over the roof of a police car. The creatures in the window were now screaming. Brad searched left and right. How did he miss that building? It was scorched and burnt like the others, but somehow the Primals found it suitable to their needs. At the base of the building where a lobby would be, the building had a gaping hole. The front windows were gone and the door long removed.

He focused his fire there and waited for the first to enter his sights before he pulled the trigger. The first shot was met with an intensity of howls and high-pitched screams. He leaned into the rifle and pulled the trigger, dropping one after another of the approaching creatures. The tow truck cranked and groaned behind him as Chelsea cussed and swore at it.

He dropped two more leaping out of the rubble of the apartment building, then shifted his aim and fired again, the bolt locking back on an empty chamber. Performing a quick magazine change, he was back on target. He heard the diesel roar to life and screech as rusted parts awoke. Chelsea's rifle joined the fight behind him as she yelled for Brad to pull back to the truck.

Squaring his hips, he moved backward while continuing to fire as he withdrew. He bumped into the already open passenger door and passed around it, piling into the truck. Sprinting creatures collided with the door, shoving it shut and trying to force their way through the open window. Brad reeled back away from their clawing hands. Chelsea was inside, her door closed. She reached over him with her pistol and fired point blank, clearing out the things to his front. The blast of the 9mm shattered his ears.

"Drive!" he screamed, pulling his own handgun and bringing it up before pulling the trigger into the faces of the creatures. The truck crashed back as it met the onslaught of Primals. He pulled the trigger until the weapon was empty, then used the head of his tomahawk to bash at and gouge the heads of the infected. Chelsea cut the wheel and worked the truck forward, crashing through the mass. The truck's heavy, cleated tires made easy work of crunching through the mess of bodies.

As the last of the creatures fell from the side of the truck, Brad leaned back into the seat, his uniform and face bloodied. Chelsea gripped the wheel with white knuckles, blood spatter covering her cheeks. She looked at him from the corner of her eye. "Are you bit?" she asked.

Brad patted at his sleeves and gloves. Pulling the shemagh from his neck, he wiped his eyes. "I'm okay."

Epilogue

The truck wound up Interstate 69, passing Fort Wayne, Indiana. Most of the road was clear, the wreckage piled and compacted into the medians. Obvious signs of a cleanup. There were painted messages from the Midwest Alliance on billboards with green arrows and directions to the safe zone. Brad drifted in and out of sleep, watching the truck break through drifts on the snow-covered highway. They passed by fields of destruction and undistinctive shapes of the wreckage.

He kept his rifle between his knees, his hand holding the barrel as his head bobbed up and down. Days of being on alert and fighting had worn him down; he knew he was at his breaking point. She reached over and squeezed his shoulder. He looked up at her with tired eyes. She pointed through a thick haze covering the highway to a sign: *Welcome to Pure Michigan;* painted in bold letters below it: *Entering the Midwest Alliance Safe Zone.*

Looking ahead, he saw the soft glow of light shining through the mist. He asked Chelsea to stop the truck and cut the headlights. With his rifle ready, he stepped out onto the highway. The night air was silent, only the low idle of the truck making any noise. His boots crunched in the snow as he stepped ahead. In the distance, the mist glowed back like a lighthouse marking the way for a lost ship.

"It goes on forever," Chelsea said, looking at the horizon.

Brad nodded his head. "As bright as the sunrise."

He moved back to the cab and closed the door behind him. Chelsea continued on, driving toward the light. The wreckage on the sides of the roads pushed back farther until eventually, it was completely removed. Two lanes of cleared highway appeared, the high grass from the median strip mowed short, only a pristine layer of snow now covering it. At a sign for a highway junction, Chelsea suddenly stopped the truck, causing Brad to look up. Where the highway connected with an east-west interstate, the road was blocked. A twelve-foot-tall wall made of concrete and steel blocked their path.

Mounted to the tops of the gray barrier were bright spotlights. One directly to their front shined brightly, flooding the wall and illuminating a sign below. A green arrow pointing left with stenciled text below it read: *Coldwater Crossing 10 miles.* Then another arrow pointing to the right, *Ann Arbor Crossing 90 miles.*

"We stay away from Ann Arbor; I'm a Spartan," Brad said, pointing to the left. Chelsea turned, driving slow and following the wall with the lights shining down over them.

The mist cleared away and they saw another search light pointed straight up into the sky, turning in small circles and marking the way. Lights on the tops of the wall began to turn and point at the tow truck.

"I think someone's up there," Chelsea said.

"Just keep going," Brad whispered. Chelsea slowed and stayed to the center of the empty road until a bright spotlight from directly ahead blinded them. Chelsea stopped the truck, her hands still frozen to the wheel.

"Brad," she said, her voice cracking.

"It's okay," he answered back. "Let's go." He put his hand to the latch and opened the door with a clunk.

She reached out and took his arm.

"It's okay," he said. Brad stepped out onto the street and closed the door behind him. He checked to see that Chelsea was doing the same. He walked to the fender of the truck and unclipped his rifle, making a show of placing it on the hood. He then did the same with his sidearm and tomahawk. He looked over to Chelsea and smiled at her. Stepping to the front of the truck, she joined him and he took his hand. Together they walked into the blinding light. He heard shouts of men and boots slapping the pavement as they moved toward them.

He felt her squeeze his hand as men in multicam uniforms emerged from the light, running toward them in two columns. The soldiers formed a line with their rifles up, but the weapons were pointed into the mist, not at them. Soon, the men moved into a rehearsed circle, surrounding them in a protective bubble as a big man with a bushy mustache entered the circle and looked Brad up and down.

Brad looked the man in the eye and extended his hand. "Sergeant Brad Thompson, United States Army."

The man grinned and answered back. "Sergeant Rufus Brown, Michigan National Guard. Welcome to the safe zone."

Thank You for reading.
Please leave a review on
Amazon.

About WJ Lundy

W. J. Lundy is a still serving Veteran of the U.S. Military with service in Afghanistan. He has over 16 years of combined service with the Army and Navy in Europe, the Balkans and Southwest Asia. W.J. is an avid athlete, writer, backpacker and shooting enthusiast. He currently resides with his wife and daughter in Central Michigan.
Find WJ Lundy on facebook:
Join the WJ Lundy mailing list for news, updates and contest giveaways.

Whiskey Tango Foxtrot Series.

Whiskey Tango Foxtrot is an introduction into the apocalyptic world of Staff Sergeant Brad Thompson.
A series with over 1,500 five-star reviews on Amazon.

Alone in a foreign land. The radio goes quiet while on convoy in Afghanistan, a lost patrol alone in the desert. With his unit and his home base destroyed, Staff Sergeant Brad Thompson suddenly finds himself isolated and in command of a small group of men trying to survive in the Afghan wasteland.

Every turn leads to danger. The local population has been afflicted with an illness that turns them into rabid animals. They pursue him and his men at every corner and stop. Struggling to hold his team together and unite survivors, he must fight and evade his way to safety.

A fast paced zombie war story like no other.

Escaping The Dead
Tales of The Forgotten
Only The Dead Live Forever
Walking In The Shadow Of Death
Something To Fight For
Divided We Fall
Bound By Honor

Praise for Whiskey Tango Foxtrot:
"The beginning of a fantastic story. Action packed and full of likeable characters. If you want military authenticity, look no further. You won't be sorry."
-Owen Baillie, Author of Best-selling series, Invasion of the Dead.

"A brilliantly entertaining post-apocalyptic thriller. You'll find it hard to putdown"
-Darren Wearmouth, Best-selling author of First Activation, Critical Dawn, Sixth Cycle

"W.J. Lundy captured two things I love in one novel-- military and zombies!"
-Terri King, Editor Death Throes Webzine

"War is horror and having a horror set during wartime works well in this story. Highly recommended!"
-Allen Gamboa, Author of Dead Island: Operation Zulu

"There are good books in this genre, and then there are the ones that stand out from the rest-- the ones that make me want to purchase all the books in the series in one shot and keep reading. W.J. Lundy's Whiskey Tango Foxtrot falls into the latter category."
-Under the Oaks reviews

"The author's unique skills set this one apart from the masses of other zombie novels making it one of the most exciting that I have read so far."
-HJ Harry, of Author Splinter

The Invasion Trilogy

The Darkness is a fast-paced story of survival that brings the apocalypse to Main Street USA.

While the world falls apart, Jacob Anderson barricades his family behind locked doors. News reports tell of civil unrest in the streets, murders, and disappearances; citizens are warned to remain behind locked doors. When Jacob becomes witness to horrible events and the alarming actions of his neighbors, he and his family realize everything is far worse than being reported.

Every father's nightmare comes true as Jacob's normal life--and a promise to protect his family--is torn apart. From the Best Selling Author of **Whiskey Tango Foxtrot comes a new telling of Armageddon.**

The Darkness
The Shadows
The Light

Praise for the Invasion Trilogy:

"The Darkness is like an air raid siren that won't shut off; thrilling and downright horrifying!" *Nicholas Sansbury Smith, Best Selling Author of Orbs and The Extinction Cycle.*

"Absolutely amazing. This story hooked me from the first page and didn't let up. I read the story in one sitting and now I am desperate for more. ...Mr. Lundy has definitely broken new ground with this tale of humanity, sacrifice and love of family ... In short, read this book." *William Allen, Author of Walking in the Rain.*

"First book I've pre-ordered before it was published. Well done story of survival with a relentless pace, great action, and characters I cared about! Some scenes are still in my head!" *Stephen A. North, Author of Dead Tide and The Drifter.*

OTHER AUTHORS UNDER THE SHIELD OF

SIXTH CYCLE
Nuclear war has destroyed human civilization.
Captain Jake Phillips wakes into a dangerous new world, where he finds the remaining fragments of the population living in a series of strongholds, connected across the country. Uneasy alliances have maintained their safety, but things are about to change. -- Discovery **leads to danger.** -- Skye Reed, a tracker from the Omega stronghold, uncovers a threat that could spell the end for their fragile society. With friends and enemies revealing truths about the past, she will need to decide who to trust. -- Sixth **Cycle** is a gritty post-apocalyptic story of survival and adventure.
Darren Wearmouth ~ Carl Sinclair

DEAD ISLAND: Operation Zulu
Ten years after the world was nearly brought to its knees by a zombie Armageddon, there is a race for the antidote! On a remote Caribbean island, surrounded by a horde of hungry living dead, a team of American and Australian commandos must rescue the Antidotes' scientist. Filled with zombies, guns, Russian bad guys, shady government types, serial killers and elevator muzak. Dead Island is an action packed blood soaked horror adventure.
Allen Gamboa

INVASION OF THE DEAD SERIES

This is the first book in a series of nine, about an ordinary bunch of friends, and their plight to survive an apocalypse in Australia. -- Deep beneath defense headquarters in the Australian Capital Territory, the last ranking Army chief and a brilliant scientist struggle with answers to the collapse of the world, and the aftermath of an unprecedented virus. Is it a natural mutation, or does the infection contain -- more sinister roots? -- One hundred and fifty miles away, five friends returning from a month-long camping trip slowly discover that death has swept through the country. What greets them in a gradual revelation is an enemy beyond compare. -- Armed with dwindling ammunition, the friends must overcome their disagreements, utilize their individual skills, and face unimaginable horrors as they battle to reach their hometown...

Owen Ballie

ZOMBIE RUSH

New to the Hot Springs PD Lisa Reynolds was not all that welcomed by her coworkers especially those who were passed over for the position. It didn't matter, her thirty days probation ended on the same day of the Z-poc's arrival. Overnight the world goes from bad to worse as thousands die in the initial onslaught. National Guard and regular military unit deployed the day before to the north leaves the city in mayhem. All directions lead to death until one unlikely candidate steps forward with a plan. A plan that became an avalanche raging down the mountain culminating in the salvation or destruction of them all.

Joseph Hansen

THE ALPHA PLAGUE

Rhys is an average guy who works an average job in Summit City—a purpose built government complex on the outskirts of London. The Alpha Tower stands in the centre of the city. An enigma, nobody knows what happens behind its dark glass. Rhys is about to find out. At ground zero and with chaos spilling out into the street, Rhys has the slightest of head starts. If he can remain ahead of the pandemonium, then maybe he can get to his loved ones before the plague does. The Alpha Plague is a post-apocalyptic survival thriller.

Michael Robertson

THE GATHERING HORDE

The most ambitious terrorist plot ever undertaken is about to be put into motion, releasing an unstoppable force against humanity. Ordinary people – A group of students celebrating the end of the semester, suburban and rural families – are about to themselves in the center of something that threatens the survival of the human species. As they battle the dead – and the living – it's going to take every bit of skill, knowledge and luck for them to survive in Zed's World.

Rich Baker

THE RECKONING

Australia has been invaded.

While the outnumbered Australian Defence Force fights on the ground, in the air and at sea, this quickly becomes a war involving ordinary people. Ben, an IT consultant has never fought a day in his life. Will he survive? Grant, a security guard at Sydney's International Airport, finds himself captured and living in the filth and squalor of one of the concentration camps dotted around Australia. Knowing death awaits him if he stays, he plans a daring escape. This is a dark day in Australia's history. This is terror, loneliness, starvation and adrenaline all mixed together in a sour cocktail. This is the day Australia fell.

Keith McArdle

GRUDGE

The United States Navy led an expedition to Antarctica in December 1946, called Operation Highjump. Officially, the men were tasked with evaluating the effect of cold weather on US equipment; secretly their mission was to investigate reports of a hidden Nazi base buried beneath the ice. After engaging unknown forces in aerial combat, weather forced the Navy to abandon operations. Undeterred, the US returned every Antarctic summer until finally the government detonated three nuclear missiles over the atmosphere in 1958. Unfortunately, the desperate gamble to rid the world of the Nazi scourge failed. The enemy burrowed deeper into the ice, using alien technologies for cryogenic freezing to amass a genetically superior army, indoctrinated from birth to hate Americans. Now they've returned, intent on exacting revenge for the destruction of their homeland and banishment to the icy wastes.

Brian Parker

49314928R00209

Made in the USA
Columbia, SC
19 January 2019